CONTENTS

I would like to acknowledge the assistance of Dermot Burns, archivist of the Royal Cork Yacht Club, formerly the Water Club of the Harbour of Cork, which was founded in 1720 and is the oldest yacht club in the world. Much of the detail on yachting comes from club records. However, the references to crews fighting over races are based on accounts from the south coast of England about that time.

1

―

THE SCHOONER

On the fifteenth day of November 1813, the schooner *Shenendoah*, an American privateer cruising for British shipping in the comfortable waters of the Caribbean, sighted the sails of a merchant brig. Her captain, Henry Veasey, immediately ordered all sail set. The brig was in the east and the sun was coming up behind her. Her sails were clear to him but it would be some minutes before the light would reach the *Shenendoah*. In that time he hoped to have gained the advantage of setting every stitch of canvas his ship could carry. He stared for a full minute at the faraway sails, his telescope pressed hard to his eye, then he shut it with a snap and turned his attention to his ship.

What he saw pleased him. Some said he was a hard-driving officer who pushed his men to near breaking point, but he was a capable man and well respected by his crew. He trained them hard, practising gunnery and sailing manoeuvres as regular as clockwork. They could gibe ship in a full gale now without losing a single sail. They ran out their guns every evening at four bells in the first dog watch – four o'clock land-time – and fired them every third day. The result of all this training was that in the few minutes from the time of sighting the sail to the moment he snapped his telescope shut, Captain Veasey's first officer, Mr Long, had made all sail without fuss or bother. Mr Long was making his way aft now, having spoken to someone about the set of the topsail, his hands folded behind his back, a look of casual interest on his face.

'Good morning to you, sir. A fine day for a chase.'

It was indeed a fine day for a chase, Captain Veasey agreed. 'We will serve out the grub, Mr Long, and then we will beat to quarters. By then we should have a pretty sharp notion of what that brig is, if she's a brig at all.'

Dónal Long brought out his own telescope and examined the sails, now well up above the horizon. 'I see what you mean,' he said. There was something funny about them, although he could not be sure what it was.

'A trick, think you, Mr Long?'

Dónal Long smiled. 'They grow desperate, sure. I have heard the governor of Cuba has put a prize on your head.' His soft Cork brogue still came through the American accent he had acquired in the course of fourteen years as a seaman in ships of that new country.

Captain Veasey growled. 'As if I was some damned pirate! Man, this is a war. Does he expect me to write to him every time I stop one of his ships?'

The captain did not expect an answer. For over a year now, the *Shenendoah* had cruised these waters. Her crew had taken seven British and one Portuguese ship and sunk another two. They had shelled Port-a-Prince and generally disrupted trade between Britain and her colonies. In return Britain had thrown a blockade around the east coast of America. Even now, they knew, British ships lay off the mouth of the Chesapeake, the *Shenendoah's* home port, blockading all trade. It was, as Captain Veasey had said, a war, and neither side was being too gentlemanly about it.

'Breakfast, Mr Long,' Captain Veasey said. 'First things first.'

An hour later the *Shenendoah* was a noisy bird winging its way over the Caribbean on her beautiful cream-coloured sails. Up and down her decks men were running out the guns, dusting down the planking with sand – partly to provide a foothold for the gun-crews and partly to soak up the blood that was sure to come – and the ship had all sail set, a cloud of canvas that strained in the moderate breeze. Ahead of them, now clearly a brig, and clearly frightened by them whatever her nationality, the prey was labouring to escape. But there would be no escape. The two ships had met in just the wrong way for that. The brig was to windward, that is to say upwind of the schooner, so her only retreat was turn and sail upwind, and that was what would decide it. The best point of sail for such a ship was in the other direction, whereas a schooner could go upwind like a bird. It was now a matter of minutes before they would be in range. Lieutenant Long stood by the helmsman, directing the course to steer but also keeping a close eye on the gun-crews as they went about their preparations.

'Kennedy, Regan, avast there. You'll overset the match-tub. Do ye want to blow us all up!'

His call brought laughter from the other gun-crews, which was made even louder by the muttered reply from Kennedy.

'Silence fore and aft!' Dónal Long called, but he did not really mean it. The crew were excited and happy and he knew that an order seriously given at this moment or any other moment would be instantly obeyed. They were, after all, Americans, and he had grown used to their ways. They would fight like lions, drink like fish, defend themselves, their friends and their country to the last drop of blood. They were fiercely proud but without an ounce of snobbery, and respected nothing except courage and seamanship. Most of them had been sailors or fishermen in the sheltered Chesapeake waters or on the wilder Atlantic before the war. Now they were dedicated and highly trained. He could trust his life to them but he was certain that if he had not been a proper seaman, if he had not shown his own courage in action, they would never have followed him as an officer.

'Carter, a touch on the sheets of that flying jib, if you please.' He could sail the ship with his eyes closed. He didn't even know what had drawn his attention to the flying jib, the highest and outermost sail on the bow, but it was not drawing well. Perhaps it was the sound. He knew the *Shenendoah* so well that he often *felt* tiny changes transmitted to him through the planking. She was a beautiful machine, taut and efficient, a sailing dream.

The captain came on deck and bade him the time of day. Then they both studied the enemy ship through their telescopes.

'What say you, Mr Long?'

'I cannot say I am happy. There's something a bit . . . troubled about her.'

'I thought so too.'

'I was only thinking, it's as if they were trying to sail her badly, to slow her down. You know the trick.'

The captain laughed and shook his head. 'Oho, don't I know it only too well.'

The trick they were talking about was a simple one. A warship, disguised as a simple cargo boat, pretends to try to escape. She sets all sail and fusses and seems to run as fast as her legs can carry her. But by one trick or another she is slowed, the crew badly trimming the sails, sailing her on too much of a heel, twisting her and turning her a little this way and that. A clever captain was just as good at making his ship go slow as he was at making her go fast. The whole idea, of course, was to lead the enemy on, to make them think they had an easy job. Once the enemy was close enough, the warship would be suddenly brisk and efficient, clearly not a cargo boat to be captured easily, but by then it would be too late.

'Why don't we try a trick of our own, Mr Long. Send a man aloft there and after a few minutes let him point away southwards and shout a lot. Make sure he can be clearly seen. Then you'll rush up into the rigging with your telescope and stare in the same direction. They'll think we've spotted something down there. That'll upset 'em. Then we'll swing off and let 'em have a broadside before we go. I'll warrant they'll come round mighty sharp and we'll see the Union Jack break out at the masthead. If not, why we'll come up to the wind again. It'll add half-an-hour to the chase, but we'll get 'em anyway!'

Five minutes later Dónal Long was reporting a 'fat treasure ship in the south' in a loud voice to the vast but silent amusement of the crew, who knew exactly what was going on. Immediately the captain began to bellow orders and the men took up their position to loosen the sails.

'Stand by the guns, now,' the captain cried. 'We'll give them something to think about before we go.' Dónal Long was at his station again, chuckling quietly. 'Bear away, Mr Long.'

'Hands to ease sheets,' Dónal Long called. 'Helm steadily now.' As the ship turned away from the wind the men began to ease the sheets, the rope that controlled the sails, to keep the maximum speed up. At the same time the captain stepped forward and said, 'Fire as she bears, my lads.'

At the same moment the first gun went off, followed quickly by the second, third, fourth and so on until all nine guns on the larboard side had been fired. The range was too great and the *Shenandoah* crew saw all nine balls land with a mighty splash between themselves and the other vessel.

Shortly they were settled on the new course, running broad before the wind towards the imaginary 'fat treasure ship'. They looked back at their enemy with interest. At first there was no change and the captain was inclined to think they had wasted their time and their shot. But Dónal Long, studying her in his telescope, pointed out that they were being watched by her officers. 'And there's a damn sight more officers than you should get in a crusty old brig like that. I bet she's waiting to see if we'll hold our course.'

Sure enough, within five minutes the brig became suddenly businesslike. The rigging swarmed with men, more men than a merchant ship should have, and the ship set even more sail as she swung round to follow them.

'Studding sails and skysails and all, by God!' said Captain Veasey. 'You were right.'

At that moment a puff of smoke in the brig's bow told them that the bow-chaser, a light gun pointing forwards, was coming into action, and sure enough they saw the ball land away on the larboard side and well behind them. 'Out of range so far.' The captain nodded. 'But not for long.'

Not for long because now their roles were reversed. The schooner was running, her worst point of sail, and the brig with her square sails and greater length was slowly inching towards them. Sooner or later they would come within range – in a matter of two hours or less at the present speed.

'We will have to fight them, Mr Long,' the captain said, and at that moment he became aware that every man on deck was looking at him.

'Aye, we will sir,' said Dónal Long. 'And won't we look a sight when we bring a British man o'war into the Chesapeake with us!'

The men all heard and suddenly they were cheering. They waved their hats over their heads and cheered and cheered until Dónal eventually shook his fist at them and cried 'Avast there! D'ye hear? Silence fore and aft! Stand to your tackles. Battle stations all!' They stopped then and turned their attention to their guns. Silence settled on the ship, except for those sounds that were so much part of their lives that they never heard them now – the creaking of ropes in blocks, the straining of the timbers, the rush of the sea.

In the silence, Captain Veasey and Dónal Long fell to planning the battle that was to come. They stood at the stern rail and gazed at the ship that was chasing them.

'She'll be unhandy,' Captain Veasey said.

'She will,' Dónal replied. He was thinking of the big square sails of the brig, the work that had to be done to brace them round, the great bulk of the hull that had to be coaxed through the water. She would not turn easily. She might miss stays in a tack, meaning that she might get stuck, unable to turn to one side or the other.

'Did you see gunports?'

Dónal shook his head. The brig was well disguised for a ship of war. He had seen no guns and no openings where the guns should be. It was a well-baited trap.

'Still, she'll have a guns a plenty.'

'Fight her now or fight her in the dark, which do you think, sir?'

The captain did not answer at first. He was weighing up their chances. It was a complicated balance. On one side was the *Shenendoah*, light, manoeuvrable, fast to windward, well drilled and well armed. On the other side was the huge weight of lead the guns of the brig could throw. She would be sure to have twenty guns a side, perhaps more, and plenty of men to work them. The British were masters of the sea. The captain of that ship would be as good at his job as Captain Veasey was at his. Still, there was no running. The shelter of the Leeward Islands was 300 away. He could hide there, if he could reach it, among the numerous tiny islands and secret anchorages. He had done it before. Under his lee was the coast of Venezuela, but that was another 200 miles away. The truth was that this English vessel would catch them up long before they sighted either shore.

'I guess we should fight 'em now, Mr Long. I'd like to have my supper in peace.'

This quiet humour was one of the things that made Dónal like his captain. He chuckled and said 'Aye aye, sir.'

They discussed the technical side of things for a while, but there was not much to be said. They had fought together many times before this.

'Very well, Mr Long. Tell the men what we will do.'

Dónal went along the single deck, talking quietly to each crew at its gun, explaining the plan to them. At each gun he met a steely determination. Each gun captain spoke for his men and said they would do their duty. When he had gone round the guns on both sides and spoken to the sailing hands as well, he came back and made his report. 'All hands ready, willing and able, sir.'

'Very good, Mr Long. You may come up.'

Dónal gave the orders that brought the ship round again. Now they were hurtling towards the enemy instead of away from it. Where before the ships were closing at a rate of inches and time seemed to stretch out before them, now they were closing so fast that time seemed to have shortened. First the crew of the *Shenendoah* could see the vague shapes of men on the upper deck. Then they could glimpse the colours they wore. Then they could see the rough shape of faces and make out the men in the foretop with their muskets.

'Steady men,' Dónal called. He did not want someone to touch off a gun by mistake now and reduce their first broadside by one ninth. 'Kissinger, give us a song!'

Big, burly bald-headed Kissinger, the German bosun's mate, still barely able to speak English but with a voice like an angel, stood out from his gun, straightened his back, clasped his arms across his chest and sang. His voice filled the ship. It was not a battle song, or a marching song, a rattling fast song that would stir the men and drive them on to terrible deeds. It was a haunting old halyard shanty about the Indian maiden and the white man who stole her. The crew took up the chorus:

O, Shenendoah, I long to hear you,
Away you rolling river,
Across that wide and stormy water,
Away, I'm bound to go,
Across the wide Missouri.

'Now, Mr Long, if you please,' Captain Veasey said. He was watching the oncoming brig, judging her speed.

Dónal Long stepped up and took the helm from the helmsman. He spun the wheel and the ship's bow paid off. The larboard guns were now pointing directly at the enemy. 'Fire as she bears!' he shouted, and immediately all the guns went off together. He did not delay to see the effect but put the wheel over again, calling out 'Sheets and braces! Let go and haul!' The *Shenendoah* came round into the wind. Now it was the starboard guns that were pointing in the right direction. The sheets were home and the sails were trimmed and drawing. *Shenendoah* was racing again. The brig had been taken by surprise. Captain Veasey told Dónal that three of the shots had struck home, one into the hull just above the waterline. But she had not expected them to turn.

The distance was closing fast now and *Shenendoah* was

going to pass very close to her enemy. If the brig turned immediately she could run them down and the collision would certainly sink the American. But her captain was not that quick, or her clumsy hull slowed her down. By the time she began to turn it was already too late. *Shenendoah* ran under her starboard side.

'Fire!'

The enormous banging of the guns; nine holes appearing in the brig's sides; the popping of musketry from the deck and rigging; then the furious faces of the officers glaring down from the quarter-deck; suddenly clear water and they were past. The *Shenendoah* had broken free to windward of the brig and now they had the upper hand.

'Hands aloft to furl the topsail.' This was the only square sail the schooner carried, useful running before the wind, but useless and awkward for the kind of work they would have to do now. They should have furled it earlier but there wasn't time.

In five minutes the British ship was wearing round to come after them again.

'Gun captains, report!' Each gun captain reported that all his men were willing and able and that the guns were loaded and run out. Dónal already knew all that, but he also knew that the ritual helped to settle the men. They liked things done by the book.

When the reporting was done he turned to the captain. 'All hands ready willing and able, sir. All guns ready.' The captain nodded. 'It's cat and mouse now, sir,' Dónal added cheerfully.

'Aye, lad. And we know that game too,' replied Captain Veasey.

'Nine shot-holes, sir! Did you see that? Every shot went home?'

'That'll trouble 'em when they tack. But how many gun-ports, Mr Long? Did you count?'

Dónal looked crestfallen. 'No sir, I was watching the fall of the shot. A great many, I think.'

The captain snorted. 'A great many, Mr Long!' He shook his head as if he could not believe that a first officer could be so vague. 'A great many! There were twelve.'

To their surprise the helmsman gave a little yelp and though they glared at him he could not hide his grin. 'Helmsman, mind your course,' the captain said mildly. 'Yes, Mr Long, she's only a twenty-four.'

Shenendoah carried eighteen guns – long nine-pounders – not a heavy armament, but accurate at long range if well-handled. If the brig had been a thirty-two – that is to say carrying thirty-two guns – then the wisest course would have been to make a run for it. But she carried only twenty-four, and that, set in the balance with *Shenendoah's* speed and handiness, would make them just about even. There was another factor which helped them too. There had been no guns run out on the brig's starboard side. The gun-ports were all open but the guns had not been run up to the breech. Dónal pointed this out.

'Quite right, Mr Long. She may not be as well manned as we thought.'

That was something. Perhaps she had taken prizes and sent some of her men away to sail them safely to port. If that were the case she would not have enough men to manage the guns on both sides and sail the ship as well. A thing like that could tip the balance in favour of *Shenendoah.*

Suddenly the fever of battle took hold of Dónal's heart. His blood raced in his head. He thought he could see everything more clearly, as if it was a crystal cold morning at home in Ireland, not a hot day on this tropical sea.

He wondered at it. What had brought him to this point, he who had left Ireland only fourteen years before, a timid boy whose only ambition was to own his own fishing smack? He supposed that life had hardened him. He had seen too much cruelty and suffered some of it himself, aye, to shirk from his duty now that there was battle in sight. In a way, he thought, his heart had died in him, that heart that had cried out against injustice so long ago. He could not now believe in the brotherhood of man as his father had taught him. He was not a better person for it, he knew. He had lost what at one time he had believed to be the best part of himself. It is all for the good, he thought bitterly. It will help my shooting. It was easier to train his guns and fire them if he did not remember that the men in front of them might once have been his friends.

2

LINE SQUALL

'Very well, Mr Long, we will try her with a broadside at long range. See to it, if you please.'

Dónal saluted the captain and went down along the waist of the ship, checking the larboard guns. He tilted them upwards so that they would carry to their furthest range.

'Request permission to try a ranging shot, sir?'

Captain Veasey considered the situation, watching the brig and chewing his upper lip. 'We'll give it away if we do,' he said simply. 'Better not.'

Dónal went back to his guns. He laid each one with greater care this time, aware of the responsibility. There would be one chance to do damage with these shots. At this range he could miss with every one. To waste precious powder and shot in a small ship like the *Shenendoah* was a serious mistake: her holds were simply not big enough to carry the kind of stores Dónal would like. Every shot should count.

'All ready, sir.'

'Very well, Mr Long. Fire when you like.'

Captain Veasey gave the order to the helmsman and the ship came round to point her guns at the brig. It was important to time the shot to perfection. They could not remain long on this course or they would give away precious ground. Equally, the English ship might decide to dodge and his shot would all go to waste. The guns had to be fired from the top of a wave, if his calculations of range were right. It was tricky, but it was what he was trained for. The captain's nerves settled and his mind went cold, all anxiety banished. He watched along the barrel of number one gun as the *Shenendoah* swung, seeing the enemy brig come into his view from his left-hand side. When it was directly in line with the barrel his senses switched to the feel of the deck and the height of the deck above the surrounding sea. He waited for one, two seconds then stepped suddenly backwards and shouted, 'Fire!'

Now the gun captains took up their part in the ballet, stepping forward with the lighted match and delicately touching the guns with the flame. A small spurt upwards – gun captains step back – a huge explosion – the guns coming back in the recoil – smoke everywhere as from a firecracker on a stage. When the wind blew the smoke out of their eyes the second part of the ballet began – crews cleaning and wetting their guns, passing the powder, the wadding, the shot. Ramming all home and running the gun out again.

While this was going on, the *Shenendoah* had come back on to her course and Dónal had the time to see what damage they had done to the brig. The lookout in the maintop called the shots. 'One, two hits. Three hits. One in their forecourse.' That was a sail braced up hard and bowsed down tight, and the hole had burst it; they could see it shredding before their eyes. 'Five splashes.'

That was eight, yet all the guns had fired. Where had the ninth shot gone? Never mind, perhaps it had gone clean over. Three hits at that extreme range wasn't too bad.

'Well done, Mr Long. We'll try again.'

Now that the brig had lost a sail it was necessary to shorten *Shenendoah*'s sail too, so as not to get too far ahead.

The crew went about the business quickly and efficiently, every man concentrating hard. They must be careful not to give away any advantage. They would not get a simple, clear shot like that again. They had surprised the brig, which had expected the *Shenendoah* to run away. They had surprised her twice and gained the tremendous advantage of two clear broadsides, both striking home. They would not take her by surprise again.

Captain Veasey was chewing his lip. 'What think you, Mr Long? How best to get another shot in.'

Dónal was excited. 'I have a plan, sir, but 'twould give away a lot of ground.'

The captain looked at him, a mischievous glint in his eye. 'Well, get it out, boy. What is it?'

'We would wear round fully, sir. Fire a full broadside, larboard guns, but instead of coming back to our course we could keep turning. Now she'll turn too, to fire at us, see, but she'll be expec8ting us to come back and that's what she'll aim for. Instead we'll keep turning and come right round to fire the starboard broadside.'

Dónal waited nervously while the captain considered the plan. A broad smile gave him his answer but when Captain Veasey clapped him on the shoulder and said 'By jingo, it's a good 'un! We'll do her. Look lively, Mr Long!' Dónal's heart leaped. He turned to the men to give the orders and was amazed to see that they were all grinning like cats at him. He should have spoken more quietly, he knew. The *Shenendoah* was too small a ship for a voice like his not to carry all over it.

When the *Shenendoah* turned for the first broadside, the brig was already turning too. Her captain was not to be taken by surprise this time. *Shenendoah* fired and almost immediately the brig fired back. It was not exactly as Dónal had planned. Some of the brig's shots struck home, one crossing the deck and killing the gun captain of the number three starboard gun. His place was immediately taken by one of the sailing hands.

But the *Shenendoah* continued her turn and here the brilliance of the strategy was proven. The English brig was now facing the wrong way and all her guns had been fired. In a few moments the *Shenendoah* rose on a wave and Dónal was frantically aiming the guns. When he stepped back, the gun captains did their work and the broadside went off smoothly. Then the *Shenendoah* carried right round and in another minute was sailing sweetly on a new course, quite out of range of the brig's cannon.

'Very well, Mr Long. Ten hits, I think.' The lookout was calling the shots as he spoke but the captain had been watching too and already knew the count. This was accuracy indeed. And the brig was suffering. There were holes visible in her sides – three at least – smoke streaming from one of the gun ports, men swarming in the rigging to remake rope that had been damaged. The attack could hardly have gone better.

Dónal smiled at his captain and the smile was returned. 'We will win this, sir,' he said.

The captain, a superstitious man, put his hand suddenly to the spoke of the wheel and touched wood. 'With God's help,' he said.

But everyone knew that if the enemy continued to chase them they could twist and turn like this all day, a shot or two at the worst hitting home each time, each shot meaning more damage, more casualties. They would see the brig striking her colours and surrendering before nightfall.

Just then a shriek from the lookout made them all look up. He was pointing northeastwards and shouting something that no one could understand. All eyes on the ship turned in that direction and a moment of horror paralysed them.

Racing towards them out of the northeast tradewinds was a black cloud on a blue sky. Beneath the cloud was a wall of rain and a straight line of the purest white water. Even at the half-mile distance they could hear that water roaring like a river in flood. It was a line squall. Such squalls were as dangerous as hurricanes, although they usually lasted for no more than a few minutes. They came roaring and screaming down on the unwary skipper, torrents of rain and shrieking winds, blinding spray. With too much sail up, as the *Shenendoah* had, no ship could withstand it. The squall would lay her over on her side with the fury of a wild animal, and in a matter of moments she would sink without a trace. By the time the squall was past the sea would be empty.

The horror lasted no more than a moment. Then Dónal and Captain Veasey were at work, fighting now for their lives, their crew and their ship. Dónal sprinted forward and himself took an axe to the main halyard. That sail came rushing down, the huge gaff that held it up falling across the shoulders of a sailor who could not get out of the way. The blow broke one shoulder and knocked the sailor unconscious. The captain had pushed the helmsman aside and was bringing the boat round into the oncoming storm. Without waiting for an order, Kennedy was letting the jib sheet fly. Someone else cut the staysail halyard and the sail came rattling down. There was no time for more. In that moment the squall was upon them and they were driven to the deck by the force of the wind and the unrelenting power of the rain. They threw themselves into what shelter they could find, huddled against the leeward bulwarks, clinging to the mast, some of them in the scuppers awash with rain and seawater.

The ship heeled over, even with so little sail still aloft. She heeled until green water flooded over the lee rail. The men scrambled out of it, knowing that to stay on the lee side might mean being washed away. They grabbed at ropes and clung to the masts. They reached hands to each other.

A cannon broke its tackle and came rushing down the deck, striking another on the far side, and together they plunged into the ocean, taking a large stretch of timber with them. A crashing sound forward told them that the foremast had gone, the only one that still carried sail. The rain was so heavy that they could not see the mast. A length of rope driven into a fury by the wind lashed across the face of a young fisherman from Tidewater, blinding him completely. The man beside him saw it happen and saw the young man let go his hold of a rope to touch his dead eyes. In an instant the wind and sea had whipped him away.

Then the squall was gone, raging away towards the English ship. The sky cleared and they were afloat on a calm sea.

Dónal and Captain Veasey surveyed the wreck that had been their beautiful schooner five minutes before. One man dead; the injured everywhere. The sails and rigging ruined, foremast gone by the board. A huge chunk of the starboard side gone completely where the cannons had broken through. Not a sail aloft, no mast fit to wear one.

They turned their eyes to the squall.

'Our only hope now is that it does as much to them,' the captain said.

'Aye, God help them,' said Dónal. He turned his attention to the ship. 'Gun captains report.' Slowly the men stood up, shocked by the awesome power of the wind. They looked about them and made their reply.

'Number one larboard, safe and sound. All hands ready, sir.'

'Number seven starboard, one man missing, sir. No powder or shot. Breaching tackle ready to break, sir.'

'Gun number three larboard, gone, sir, plain gone ... '
And so it continued. No one shouted. No one complained. It was the steadying drill that they were used to. The captain would need this report before he could start to plan their next move. He would need to know the loss and damage.

But all eyes were turned towards the squall. Any moment now the English brig would emerge from it and the state she was in would tell them immediately what their fate would be – escape or surrender. If she was badly mauled it might still be an equal contest: which of them could make enough sail to escape. Or perhaps, caught with her canvas up she might have capsized completely, or lost all her masts. That was the hope.

The great curtain of rain trailed along. The water boiled underneath it. It seemed to Dónal that a grey shape could be made out within it, very like a ship. The shape became clearer and suddenly the rain was past and the brig was there, heaving and rolling. She had not a scrap of sail aloft. Instead thin strips of canvas fluttered from the spars. Every single sail had been blown out by the storm. But her masts were still standing and that, Dónal knew, was the end of the *Shenendoah* , because it would not be hard to put new sail on, but Captain Veasey could never make a new foremast. In an hour or two they would be prisoners. He looked up at the masthead for the great dark flag he had come to love, the good old stars and stripes, but it was gone, blown away like everything else in five minutes at the mercy of the elements. There would be no striking of colours, no flag fluttering sadly downwards to say 'We surrender'. That was something, anyway.

'Mr Long, I see the dory is still safe and sound. Make yourself a white flag and row over there to offer our surrender. And ask them if we can render any assistance.'

Captain Veasey was already going below. Dónal knew he would bundle all his charts, his notes and logbooks into a bag weighted with grapeshot. When he emerged on deck again he would simply drop it over the side, lest it fall into the hands of the enemy. Captain Veasey would not need the charts of his beloved Chesapeake region for many a long year.

Dónal turned to his work and in a short time he was sitting in the stern of the dory being rowed across. The sea was suddenly still after all the noise of battle and storm. The water was like a glass in which Dónal could see the boat and the oars mirrored. Ahead of him was captivity, years as a prisoner of war in some grey English city. The brig, which he could now identify as the *Lion*, meant nothing to him now but defeat and despair. He did not look at it. Instead he stared downwards into the sea and saw only his own gloomy face, distorted by the ripples, staring back at him.

3

THE PRISONER

Dónal and Captain Veasey were stalking up and down the maindeck, trying not to get in the way of the sailors going about their business, and swinging their arms in a vain attempt to get warm. Already it was winter in the cold North Atlantic. An hour before, a lookout had hailed the quarterdeck with the news that there was land on the larboard bow, but for the life of them neither Dónal nor the captain could make it out. Low cloud and occasional drizzle hid almost everything except the oak planking under their feet, the ship, her crew, her sails and the cold dark waters of the Atlantic.

Their captivity had not been harsh. They were confined in a cabin by night but had the run of the deck by day, except that if the ship had to go to action stations they would be imprisoned in the orlop, the lowest deck on the ship. The men also got their exercise and there had been no bad treatment. Only two men had been pressed into the Royal Navy – Kennedy and Regan, both of whom had Irish ancestors. Pressing was common. There was no blame attached to either side. One benefit was that

Kennedy and Regan brought them scraps of news from time to time. Unfortunately they could not navigate and no one would tell them what their destination was.

'It has to be England,' Dónal was saying.

'What does it matter, Mr Long? It's a prison ship for us!'

'Never,' Dónal said, genuinely shocked. 'Never think it, Captain Veasey! For shame, the British will not confine American officers in a prison hulk!'

'Indeed they will not!' said a hearty voice behind them. They turned to see the first lieutenant, Mr Congreve, a bluff man with a loud voice. He was the one to meet Dónal when he first came to surrender and Dónal had been impressed by his kindness. Instead of cursing him or shouting at him, the man had saluted smartly and said, 'My compliments sir. I have never seen a ship fought so brilliantly!' Dónal had almost broken down and cried at that.

And Mr Congreve had been like that ever since. He had frequently invited the American officers to dine in the officers' wardroom, and had confided in Dónal that he too had Irish ancestry.

The Irish part of Dónal's name had been a problem at first. If Dónal was an Irishman he was actually a British citizen, and if he was fighting for America, then he was a traitor and despite all their regrets and so forth, he must be hanged from a yardarm at the earliest opportunity. They were very sorry of course, deeply sorry, but that was the law. Fortunately Dónal had his papers which showed him to be an American citizen and this had come as a great relief to the British, who assured him they had no desire to hang so gallant an officer.

The next problem had been the status of the ship. She was not of the American navy? Then perhaps she was a pirate, in which case they would be obliged to hang the entire ship's company. A most distressful situation. They were very worried by that for a time, until Captain Veasey produced the ship's letter of marque, a document which authorised them to behave as if they were in the navy. Even now, Dónal remembered Captain Veasey reading the letter in his strongest 'quarterdeck voice':

BE IT KNOWN, That in pursuance of an act of congress, passed on the 26th day of June one thous-and eight hundred and twelve, I have commission-ed, and by these present do commission, the private armed Schooner called the Shenendoah, *mounting eighteen carriage guns, and navigated by one hundred & nine men, hereby authorising Nicholas Veasey captain, and Daniel Long, lieutenant of the said Schooner and whatsoever other officers and crew thereof, to subdue, seize, and take any armed or unarmed British vessel, public or private. This commission to continue in force during the pleasure of the President of the United States for the time being.*

GIVEN under my hand and seal of the United States of America, at the City of Washington.

By James Madison, the President.
Jas. Monroe Secretary of State.

There was no quarrelling with that. The British officers had relaxed and turned to the business of sorting out the damage to the ship. From then on Dónal and his comrades were prisoners of war and got a fair treatment.

Now here was Lieutenant Congreve reassuring them that they would not finish up in a prison hulk. 'And the captain's compliments to you gentlemen,' he said. 'Would you care to dine with him this evening?'

They accepted with pleasure.

Normally the captain kept a good table but now there was not much food left to eat, the ship having cruised in the Caribbean and crossed the Atlantic. They had eaten pretty well everything on board so there was nothing left but salt beef and weevilly biscuit. But there was still plenty of drink.

They had consumed a vast quantity of wine and now had started on several bottles of port. The company consisted of Captain Pye, Lieutenant Congreve, Second Lieutenant Whitlock, Mr Thomas the master, Captain Veasey and Dónal. Quite early in the meal Lieutenant Whitlock had given in to the effects of wine, which he confessed he was not accustomed to, and had asked permission to leave the table. This was granted, and shortly afterwards the master Mr Thomas excused himself on the grounds that he had work to do. Again the captain excused him.

Now it was just the two captains and the two first officers. The bottle of port passed from hand to hand and the conversation became more lively. Until now the men had been friendly enough but the alcohol was having its effect and tempers were rising.

Captain Veasey had made the mistake of referring to an old friend of his, Captain Thomas Boyle. He did not notice the annoyance that the mention of his name caused the English officers. Thomas Boyle was an American ship's captain who had done a great deal of damage to British navy vessels since the outbreak of war. Captain Veasey went on to quote Boyle's famous saying that 'His schooner had been chased by thirty-four different British frigates and brigs of war and she had always outsailed 'em.' He laughed loudly at his own story and looked around the company to see if the others laughed too. Instead he met Captain Pye's stony glare.

Captain Veasey was disappointed with the reaction of his English hosts and he had drunk enough wine and port to tell them so. 'Goddarn po-faced rogues!' he said, a remark which had a very poor effect on Captain Pye.

'A veritable pirate!' was the reply. 'Boyle is a veritable pirate!'

'The man is a personal friend,' Captain Veasey declared. 'Fine sailor and a darned good . . . ' He seemed to forget what he was going to say. 'A darned good man on a horse.' The last point did not seem to have any impact so he developed it further. 'Never saw a sailor could sit a horse like him.'

Dónal tried to change the subject. 'Excellent port, Captain, if I may say so.'

'Yes, capital, sir.' Lieutenant Congreve doing his bit.

'Thank you.'

'A toast, sir?' Captain Veasey was rising unsteadily to his feet. He banged his head off the timbers and remembered suddenly that he was still on board a ship. He sat down again, contenting himself with lifting his glass. 'To Thomas Boyle, the best darned horseman I ever saw!'

They all drank to that.

'Dashed silly war anyway,' Captain Pye said and hiccuped into his glass. 'Pardon me.'

'Agreed,' said Captain Veasey. 'Your fault.'

'America declared it!'

'Had to,' said Captain Veasey. 'You kept pressing men out of our ships.'

'Necessities of war, Captain.'

'The *Shannon*...' A few years before a British frigate, the *Shannon*, had fired into an American ship called the *Chesapeake* because she would not give up sailors who were born in England. Twenty-three men were killed. The incident had caused outrage in America and shame in England. 'That darned *Shannon* murdered our boys...'

Captain Pye did not bat an eyelid. 'Colonies,' he said.

Captain Veasey blinked. 'Beg pardon?'

'Dashed colonies! Fight one's own colonies... rubbish!'

Captain Veasey attempted to rise again and gave himself a second knock on the head. 'Ouch,' he said. 'United States of America!'

'Never trust natives,' Captain Pye said. His head was beginning to droop and his voice was becoming indistinct. But Captain Veasey understood well enough. He began to sing in a toneless mumble:

Fired our guns an' the British kep a runnin,
Down Mississippi to Gulf Mexico...

His voice trailed off. The two captains glared at each other for a moment, then Captain Pye roused himself to be hospitable again. He lifted his glass. 'Confusion to our enemies!' A broad smile suggested to the Americans that he did not mean them. They drank.

'Dashed Bonaparte,' he said. 'Pass the port, old boy.'

'Boney's not the worst of 'em,' Captain Veasey replied, wagging his finger in the air as if the Englishman was a bold schoolboy. 'Know where you are with Boney. Better'n old King George.'

Captain Pye had dozed off in the space of two seconds but now his head jerked up. 'Red Indians,' he said, and everyone, even Captain Veasey was confounded by that.

Shortly afterwards, the two lieutenants were able to slink away to the quarterdeck, leaving their captains quarrelling drunkenly about the recent American invasion of Canada.

On the quarterdeck they leant on the rail and watched the dark sea streaming past. That was the only sound apart from the murmured conversation between the officer of the watch and the helmsman.

'See the lights, my friend?' Lieutenant Congreve said. Dónal had been watching them since he came on deck. 'Home, eh?'

Dónal flared up suddenly, angry at his captivity, angry at the war, angry at Lieutenant Congreve for assuming that Dónal would see England as home. 'Home for me? Certainly not. That country has been the cause of so much grief in Ireland! How could I see your England as home?'

Lieutenant Congreve looked strangely at him. 'England? What of England? That is not our destination.

We are bound for Ireland. You will be home before long. Home in Ireland.'

Dónal gaped at him. 'Ireland?'

Now Lieutenant Congreve smiled broadly. 'Ireland it is.'

Dónal clasped his hand and shook it warmly. 'This is good news. Oh, so much better than prison in a strange country!'

'Better prison at home, eh?'

Dónal thought for a moment before answering. 'Home,' he said, wondering at the word. 'I suppose it is. But I was only twelve when I left, you know. I guess I've grown used to America since then. Anyway, you know very well, Congreve, that a sailor's home is his ship.'

'Quite right, quite right. Still – the exile's return and all that.'

'I never expected to return a prisoner.'

'Ah yes, but a prisoner of war! There's the thing. An honourable prisoner who fought magnificently. Why, but for that squall Captain Pye and I would have been prisoners in Chesapeake Bay long ago!'

'You've said so a hundred times, but it is not so. That squall *did* happen, and I am your prisoner. I will go home a prisoner and there's no denying it.'

Lieutenant Congreve was a kindly man and he and Dónal had become friends over the weeks of the voyage. 'Look, old boy, you'll get parole. I'll see to it. You'll be free as a bird.' A sudden thought crossed his mind. 'You would accept parole? You would give your word not to escape?'

'I think so,' Dónal said. 'It's a long way to America anyway. I'd never swim it!'

'We'll be putting in at the Cove of Cork. Do you know it?'

Dónal was delighted. 'The Cove of Cork! Why, I spent all my childhood looking at it. I was born just across the bay.'

They watched the lights in silence for a time.

Lieutenant Congreve jerked his thumb in the direction of the captain's cabin. 'He can't take his drink. Would you believe that sober he is the best captain a man could wish for. I'm sorry you were subjected to that . . . that exhibition.'

'Don't apologise for it,' Dónal told him. 'Anyway, look at old Veasey. He's as bad. Would *you* believe that he is a prime seaman?'

'I do believe it – I know it. I saw the way that schooner was handled. We were all amazed.'

They discussed the battle. Apparently Captain Pye had planned a trick of his own – a fake fire, the ship caught in irons, hands running around 'like headless chickens' as he said. 'Would that have caught you?'

'I think so,' Dónal said. He did not say that they would have stood off so that the broadside could not be brought to bear on them. That in their time as privateers they had seen and used almost every trick imaginable. That the *Shenendoah* could have outsailed the English brig and sunk her without even coming within the field of fire of her broadside. It would be churlish to point any of that out. He was coming to look on 'Old Congreve', as he called him, as something of a friend. He called him 'Old Congreve' out of affection, as he called Captain Veasey 'Old Veasey'. Congreve was, in fact, only six years older than himself.

'Have you been to Cork before?' Dónal changed the subject. The memory of the loss of the *Shenendoah* was still painful to him.

'Yes. Once. In '98. You remember that business. I was a midshipman in the *Hornet*.'

Suddenly Dónal was cold. He shivered deeply and shook his shoulders. He remembered that 'business' very well. The year of 1798. English and French armies in the field, hundreds of thousands of rebels driving over the land like a huge wave. Torture and murder. Incredible courage and incredible foolhardiness. All the great ideals of his childhood – unity of purpose, liberty, an end to religious intolerance. It was his past, he knew, yet he dared not think about it. He said, 'I must go below and fetch my boat cloak . . . on second thoughts, perhaps I should turn in.'

'Yes,' Lieutenant Congreve agreed. 'We've had too much to drink.' But as he watched Dónal going towards the ladder, he was thinking that it was a funny thing, the way the man had shaken with cold at the very mention of '98.

'He could hardly have been a rebel,' he thought. 'Certainly he would have been too young? What then? Well, time will tell no doubt.' He yawned and stretched, glanced at the quartermaster at the wheel out of habit, tipped his hat to the officer of the watch and went to bed.

When Dónal got to his cabin Captain Veasey was already in his cot, snoring his head off. Dónal slipped quietly into bed and lay there, his hands clasped behind his head, thinking about his destination.

By now, so many years later, the trouble of the rebellion should have died down. There would be no one seeking a boy who had grown up and turned his back on politics. He was not afraid. In a way he was glad. At least he would not be in England, where he knew no one and where he would always be simply an enemy. But Ireland was the country he had left behind, the land he had dreamed of leaving, with its cruel landlords, its brutal soldiers, its devious and callous government. In America they called it 'the old country'. And in his own memory it was old and worn out. America on the other hand was young and exciting. The air was free and there was no landlord to raise the rent or turn him out on the road, not at least in the world of the Chesapeake Bay shipping companies. If you worked hard you could make your way. He had grown used to that.

Now, whether he wanted to or not, he was going back.

He would stay out of politics, though – no truck with whatever rebellions were brewing there now, no secret societies, no plots. He would steer clear of all that and when this war was over he would be sent back to America and he would resume his career. That was his plan.

4

HOME

It was a cold grey dawn when Dónal Long sighted the battered old lighthouse at Roche's Point, where he had taken his departure fourteen years earlier on board the *Provident of Boston*. It was an ill-starred journey, for the ship that he believed would save him and take him to America to learn his trade as a seaman turned out to be a slave-trader. Those were the worst days of Dónal's life, worse even than these days as a prisoner because now at least he knew he had done his duty and behaved like a man of honour.

So it was with mixed feelings that he saw the lighthouse beam dimming in the morning light. It brought back memories he would have liked to forget – the death of his parents, the bullying of his uncle, the cruel days of the rebellion, the death of his first true friend Charlie Madden. And then there was that horrific journey south to the African coast, made even worse when the slaves were brought aboard. No, he could not, would not, think about those days. He had put that time behind him. He had reached America with a second friend, good Davey Burgess, who had taught him navigation and got him a place

in a trading schooner – who had put him on the right road.
And once Dónal's foot was on that road, he had stepped
along it with care but with a free heart. He had risen in
his trade. He had volunteered to fight for his new country
against the old enemy and he had fought honourably and
well. In a few years he would captain his own ship, he was
certain of it. That would be the fulfilment of all his
dreams. It was an ambition that was within his sights.

And he was certain also that this war would not last. It was
a foolish and artificial war anyway. Soon the American and
British governments would come to their senses and make
peace. Dónal Long made up his mind he would be gone on the
next packet ship for America when that day came. Ireland was
not for him. It held nothing but bad memories.

Still, his heart leaped to see the old cottage standing on the
hill above Ballymonas and the masts of fishing boats bobbing
in the quiet bay. When they rounded the Spit and turned for
Cove his heart lifted at the sight of the old town, still clinging
to the edge of the sea and the side of the hill at the same time.
His mind was filled suddenly with memories and the words of
a song he thought he had forgotten:

> *We entered the harbour, we rounded the Spit,*
> *We landed at Cove all able and fit . . .*

He struggled to recall the rest of the words.

'So this is your old country, Mr Long?' Captain Veasey
had been looking pale all day, and had kept to his bunk as much
as he could. Now he was standing by Dónal's side without so
much as a word about his drunken behaviour last night. Dónal
decided to be cool with him.

'It is, sir.'

'Pretty fine anchorage, Mr Long? Handsome place.' Captain Veasey was trying to be nice, to make up for disgracing himself.

'So they say.' Not an inch. Dónal would make him feel it.

'Did you sleep well? Last night, I mean.'

'Perfectly.' Dónal had, in fact, slept very little – what with his own worries and Captain Veasey's snoring.

The captain was silent but Dónal could hear him drawing short rapid breaths. He was obviously trying to control his temper. He failed, though. 'Goddarn Irish! Listen to me.' He grabbed Dónal's arm and pulled him round to face him. 'Listen here, sonny boy. I'm your captain and I'm entitled to get drunk if I want, and it's no business of yours. Now what do you make of that, Mr Long?'

'I was only thinking, sir, that you let your country down.'

The captain exploded. 'By God it's mutiny! If I was aboard the *Shenendoah* I'd see you swing for that remark sir! I'd see you swing, I would!' He was shouting, and the noise had attracted a grinning crowd of British sailors and American prisoners. 'Put up your fists, damn you!' The captain stood back and stuck his fists out in the attitude of a professional prizefighter. 'In my day a man had to fight to be an officer! By God, I've beaten many an awkward mate before this! Put up your dukes, I say! Put 'em up!'

Captain Veasey often called him 'mate', which in a merchant ship was the same rank as lieutenant. But this time he was using it as a term of insult.

The sailors were shouting encouragement but in spite

of himself, Dónal had to smile as he remembered again why he had grown to like Captain Veasey so much over the past two years. Instead of putting up his fists he held out his hand. 'Shake hands, Captain. We may not meet again until the war is over,' he said.

The words completely disarmed the old captain, who also dropped his fists. 'Goddarn Irish,' he said, but he shook Dónal's hand, tears in his eyes. 'You're right, son. I let the country down.'

'No, sir,' said Dónal. 'Only I am angry with everything at present and I blamed you.'

Just then the bosun's mate came down the deck, swinging his rope-end right and left and calling for the watches to take their stations for mooring. Dónal and Captain Veasey shook hands warmly again. 'I'll see you in Baltimore, State of Maryland, son,' the captain said.

'There's a Baltimore here too,' Dónal replied. 'The first one.'

'Is that a fact?'

'But I'll see you anyway, Captain.'

Dónal and Captain Veasey were marched at the head of the *Shenendoah's* crew down the gangplank and on to the quay at Cove. A company of marines shepherded them into a corner and stood guard over them while they waited for the soldiers who were to take them away. The captain and Dónal were not to be parted after all. They were all to be imprisoned in a fort, the men in a disused barracks, the two officers in a spare room in the barrack square.

Dónal was painfully embarrassed at being herded on to the quay in full view of his countrymen – and countrywomen, for a lot of the ladies of the town, who had been promenading on the fashionable Columbine Quay, made their way over to the dock to view the 'wild Americans', as one lady called them. Worse, however, was the portly woman who referred to them as 'savages' and spat at them when no one else was looking.

But consolation was to be found in the small group of younger women who, instead of scorning, pitied them. Dónal heard one young lady say, 'What the poor gallants must have endured,' and 'Such courage to fight our navy in their cockle-shell ships'. He made up his mind that if he were released on parole in Cove he would keep a weather eye open for this girl and tell her, if he could, how much her words had eased his shame. And also, maybe, point out to her that the *Shenendoah* was far from a 'cockle-shell' but a trim fighting schooner.

Then a company of infantry in their scarlet coats came tramping down the hill and along the waterfront. Much saluting and compliments between them and the marines, much shouting of orders, stamping of feet, presenting of arms and saluting again, and the Americans were once more under way, tramping through the town and out a little distance into the country.

In the end, they found themselves in a small fort at a point which Dónal recognised as Carrignafoy, near Cuskinny. If he looked eastward he could see Ballymonas Bay where he grew up. To the north were thick woods.

'It is not such a bad place,' he told himself. 'It is not as bad as a ship in a storm.'

Captain Veasey settled in too. They had a room of their own. They could exercise in the camp by day, although by night they were locked in. They were wakened in the morning by the trumpeter blowing reveille and the ceremony of lowering the flag at sunset was the signal that they would be imprisoned again. Their room was spacious and the exercise yard at least had a view of the sea.

'It's about the size of a goodly brig,' Captain Veasey said of their room. 'And a darn sight drier!'

'Aye,' said Dónal, shivering as an icy gust blew under the door and rattled the windows. 'But it's just as cold.'

The days wore on. Dónal got to know the officers and they brought him what news they had. Since *Shenendoah* had been at sea several months at the time she was captured, he and the captain did not know, for example, that Napoleon had been heavily defeated at Leipzig in October, or that by now the Allies were marching on Paris. This was bad news, because if Napoleon was defeated the British would be able to concentrate on America. Better news, however, came from America itself. Admiral Perry had defeated the British fleet on Lake Erie in September ('Good old Perry!' Captain Veasey said. 'A great admiral and a darn fine cardplayer!') and the British army had been defeated at the Battle of the Thames. The great Indian chieftain Tecumseh, who had supported the British, had been killed there. Less satisfactory was the news that the daring American attack on Montreal, down the St Lawrence river and around Lake Champlain, had failed.

Time passed slowly. The officers' quarters were bare and chilly, although an orderly came in at noon every day and lit a fire for them. The two friends were glad when winter wore into spring. They played chess on a board lent them by the quartermaster and read while they had light. Dónal gave Captain Veasey a course in Irish history and the American soon learned some Irish songs. It was strange for Dónal to hear the old words in the accent of the New World. He wondered what the drawing rooms of Baltimore and Boston would make of Captain Veasey's Irish sentiments when he came home after the war.

One day Dónal was summoned to the commanding officer. 'Sit down, Long,' the bewhiskered colonel said. He looked at some papers on his desk and said, 'You are Irish, Long?'

'Aye, sir. I was born here . . . But I'm an American citizen now,' Dónal added hastily.

'Yes, yes, we know that.' The fact seemed to irritate the colonel. 'They could have pressed you into the navy, you know. They've pressed other so-called Americans.'

'I understand that this is what the war is all about, Colonel. The fact that Britain will not leave our seamen in their ships.'

'By God! That's impertinent, sir! *Our* seamen, by God.'

'I am an American.'

The colonel controlled his temper. 'They'll always be colonies to me. I mean to say, the tea business was wrong, but still, they may call themselves Americans, they'll always be colonists to me.'

Dónal held his tongue this time. The colonel was not a bad sort and not too long before he had lent Dónal some books. Now he coughed and fixed his gaze on the window. He looked very uncomfortable.

'We could use someone like you, Long. At least, the navy chappies could. Someone who knows the lie of the land. I may as well tell you there's something brewing in that Chesapeake area. That's where your ship came from, isn't it? A bit of a show. You could be very useful there. I should think there'd be a commission in it for you.'

Dónal considered what he was being asked. It was tempting. It would get him out of prison. It would get him back to sea as an officer, probably a junior lieutenant. *And* the war would certainly be over soon.

But it was only a momentary temptation. There was no honour in changing sides. He was a prisoner of war and that is how he would remain unless an American ship came into the harbour and rescued him, which was most unlikely. He had never betrayed a trust or a friendship and he would not do so now. He would not become a spy or a traitor.

'I'm afraid I couldn't do that, sir.'

The colonel looked relieved. He actually smiled for a brief moment. 'Yes, yes. Of course you couldn't. I quite understand. No honourable man would accept such an offer. I would say the same myself.' He and Dónal looked at each other with respect. 'Well, Long, is there anything you or Captain Veasey require?'

'No, sir. Thank you. Except, perhaps, news of our men?'

'Oh, they're all right. They complain a bit.'

'They always do.'

'Do they?' The colonel seemed amazed by the fact. 'British seamen never do.'

Not half, thought Dónal, as he was led away. The colonel should have been on the lower gundeck of the old *Leander!*

Not long afterwards the colonel spoke to Dónal and Captain Veasey about parole. This was a system whereby a prisoner gave his solemn word of honour that if released he would not try to escape or work against his captors in any way. If Dónal and Captain Veasey gave him their word, the colonel said, he was authorised to give them parole between the hours of dawn and sunset. They must, of course, report back to the camp before the evening gun. This was quite a common arrangement, the officers being on their word of honour to behave decently, and the parole was very rarely broken.

Dónal enquired why they were suddenly being granted this favour and the colonel told them that a Lieutenant Congreve had annoyed the Admiralty office until they agreed to allow the parole.

Dónal and Captain Veasey accepted the terms gratefully and the following day found them going their separate ways through the bustling streets of Cove.

5

ACHILLES DAUNT

The elderly gentleman making his way through the traffic of the dockside could have been any merchant making his living in the busy port. He stopped from time to time and spoke to other gentlemen, or tipped his hat to such ladies as dared to take their walk among the dockers, sailors, naval officers, merchants, crimps and tavern criers. There was something old-fashioned in his bearing and in the gallant and exaggerated bow he made to the ladies. It was probably this that attracted the attention of the cutpurse who watched him as he made his way on to the recently built Columbine Quay. This cutpurse, a sly-faced boy of about fifteen, fell into step behind him and followed him along the walk, waited patiently while he spoke to someone he had agreed to meet and then followed him back again, along the wharf past the moored ships.

At last his patience was rewarded. A young woman was sitting propped against a stone bollard. She was obviously one of the hundreds of people who had fallen on hard times in recent years – the wife of a small tenant farmer who had died, or who had perhaps been caught up in the uprising of some years before. The gentleman seemed to speak kindly to her and the cutpurse could see that the young woman looked on him as a benefactor. The gentleman reached inside his heavy cloak and produced a small leather bag. At that moment, the cutpurse slipped his double-bladed knife from his sleeve into the palm of his hand. As the gentleman dipped his fingers to take out a coin he felt the strings that bound the purse to his waist loosen. He barely saw the flash of the blade that cut them before the purse was gone.

He stared foolishly at his hand, then at the woman, whose jaw hung down in shocked surprise. He turned in time to see a shadowy figure running into a side-street.

'Thief!' he shouted. 'Stop thief!' His legs were too weak to propel him into a run but he was heartened to see that some men were already in pursuit. He turned to the woman with his palms turned up as much as to say, 'You see? I have nothing to give you now.'

Dónal Long was running as fast as his legs could carry him, weaving among the carts, the strollers, the hawkers, the merchants, the fine ladies, the beggars, the dockmen carrying boxes and bales, the soldiers and sailors on shore leave. The thief was fast but he was tiring, and Dónal, revelling in the exercise that had been denied him these past months, was slowly catching up.

Now the thief's path was taking him up the winding hills that backed the little waterside town and the pressure was telling on him. He could hear the sound of his pursuer's boots echoing in the still air and he knew he would have to turn and fight. He carried his double-bladed knife still but he had never had to use it in anger. It was one thing to be taken as a thief: the sentence would be Cork Gaol, or perhaps transportation to New South Wales, but if once he used that knife he could face a gallows. Across his mind flashed the images of three bodies dangling from the hanging holes on the front wall of Cork Gaol. He had gone there once to see a hanging but he had been late, and when he got there the condemned men were already dead. Nevertheless he had stared in horror for over an hour.

He stopped at a corner where the streets crossed in a T-shape. Here he turned and faced the pursuer. They stared at each other for a moment, then the pursuer came slowly forward.

'Stop where you are,' the thief said, and to emphasise the words he flashed his dagger from his sleeve into the palm of his hand. 'I got a dirk. I cut many a man before you. I'll cut your throat.'

Dónal laughed. 'You're a cutpurse not a cut-throat, mister. Anyway, I've faced worse than that little blade in my time.'

The thief eyed his threadbare foreign uniform and guessed that what the young man said was true. For a moment he thought of running again but he realised that he could not escape.

Dónal, advancing slowly, step by step, was now almost within striking range, and the thief darted the dirk at him, almost invisible in its speed except for the sudden flash of sunlight on the blade. 'Stand or I strike!'

Dónal stopped sharp. He had no desire to die with that vicious little blade in his heart. 'I'll make a bargain with you,' he said. The thief's eyes narrowed. 'You give me that purse and I'll let you go. That's fair.'

'I'd make a fretwork of you rather than give you that purse.'

'I don't have the time to talk. You'd better start, I reckon.' Dónal's smile was broad and relaxed.

The thief glanced quickly right and left, then made as if to run. Dónal stepped forward and the blade darted out, nicking the sleeve of his left forearm. The thief was already turning to the left. Just two steps carried him out of Dónal's reach but the third step brought him down flat on his face. He had not noticed that an open drain crossed the street at that point and his toe had caught in the edge. He was up almost immediately but before he could run again he felt a stinging blow on the back of his head. His blade was out again and he turned to face his attacker, but he turned into the full force of a swinging fist. He stumbled backwards, almost losing his balance.

There was noise from behind him and out of the corner of his eye he could see at least two men cautiously approaching his back. He made a quick decision, reached into his coat with his free hand, produced the purse, held it up to Dónal and pitched it at his face. Dónal caught it and in that instant the thief was past him, running along the other side of the street. At the first chance he turned right, and went down the hill at breakneck speed. A sudden left again and he was gone.

Dónal stood in the sunshine, staring at the bag of coins. His heart was still racing from the pleasure of action after so long a confinement. He looked up at the men who had come to help him and laughed, and they laughed too and praised him, and suddenly their familiar accents and their ready smiles told him that he was, after all, at home.

Dónal thanked the two strangers for coming to his aid and made his way slowly down the hillside streets, past the thatched cottages of fishermen and the slate-roofed shops down to the quayside again. He found the gentleman still standing on the quay, explaining to yet another passer-by how he had been robbed that very morning in broad daylight.

'I believe this is your purse, sir,' Dónal said.

The gentleman was astonished . . . never expected to see his money again . . . quite taken aback at the young man's goodness . . . grateful, extremely grateful. Dónal felt the man's eyes examining his worn old uniform and his pale face.

'I must reward you, sir,' he said. Dónal shook his head. 'I beg of you to accept some small token . . . ' Again Dónal shook his head.

'I would do the same for my worst enemy, sir.'

'I must entreat you to sup with me then. A bite of dinner. I was on my way to Aeneas Lane's eating-house. I pray you, eat a bite in my company.'

Hunger – for real food, not the slops the army fed him – suddenly assailed Dónal. He hesitated a moment, out of good manners, then agreed, and very shortly he and the gentleman were seated in the window table at Aeneas Lane's watching the crowds going by.

'My name is Daunt. Achilles Daunt, sir, merchant and ship-owner. If I may be of service to you, I should be glad of it.' They shook hands.

'Dónal Long, sir. First officer of the privateer schooner *Shenendoah*, until we lost her off the Leeward Islands back in the fall of last year. At present resident in Carrignafoy Fort.'

They had ordered food and now the serving boy brought two heaped plates of mutton chops and an enormous side-plate of potatoes and cabbage.

Achilles Daunt watched as his companion devoured the food. When Dónal's hunger was partly satisfied he looked up and met the old man's amused eyes. He blushed as he remembered his manners.

'I beg your pardon sir,' he said. 'But you see, I have been dining on what the army calls food for some months, and before that I was some time at sea. Now you know sir, that at sea we do not think of food at all. Ship's biscuits with weevils asleep in them. Bread with cockroaches parading up and down on it like fine ladies on Sunday afternoon. Beef that you could make boots out of. Brackish water that tastes like a mixture of oak barrels, Stockholm tar and bog. That has been my diet this past year more or less. Mutton chops are new to me.'

They laughed together at his description.

'I see that this old Cove of Cork has become prosperous since I was last here in '98.'

Achilles Daunt looked closely at his guest when he mentioned the year '98, but concluded that the lad was too young to have fled the disturbances of that time. Many who had been out with pike and gun in that year were beginning to come back, believing that the law no longer looked for them.

'Indeed, you will see changes, here, Mr Long. Many men of

substance have been busy. I instance Mr Smith Barry who owns much of the town here and he has taken it as his duty to raise the commercial status of Cove. He has built that handsome promenade at the western end and named it after his pleasure-yacht *Columbine*. A very fine yacht. Perhaps you are familiar with the vessel?'

Dónal Long shook his head. The notion of a pleasure-yacht was quite foreign to him. There was no time for such frippery in the Chesapeake.

'And his designs have been much advanced by the navy, who moved their victualling yards from Kinsale to Haulbowline Island in the year three so that a considerable portion of the beef and salt butter on His Majesty's ships comes from the Cove of Cork now. I may tell you that between August and January of this year alone, 90,000 of fat cattle have been slaughtered here for that trade.' Dónal whistled in surprise. 'You are astonished? What would you say to 60,000 barrels of grain, 70,000 barrels of pork, 1,300,000 yards of plain cloth? We quite prosper here in Cork.'

Dónal Long said he was very glad to hear it and hoped that the whole country prospered too, for it had been in a sad way when he left it some years ago.

But at this, Achilles Daunt's face became downcast. Since the Act of Union had gone through parliament, he told Dónal, there had been nothing but hardship for poor Ireland and industry was quite stifled. 'To be sure, agriculture profits by it, for it is said Ireland is the granary of the Empire. But His Majesty's government has seen fit to tax our industry to death.'

'Indeed,' said Dónal, 'That is how they lost their colonies in the New World. It seems they will never learn. And I have seen hundreds of poor men and women begging in the by-streets.'

'And thousands more await the emigrant ship. There are landlords who are shipping their tenants to Australia merely in order to graze sheep on the land where people live. Here in the town we do not see it. We are protected. But to take a carriage into the country is to see true poverty.'

Their speech had become a little muffled as they started again on what was left of the mutton chops and Dónal's hunger prevented him from making any further enquiries. He devoured, in all, six chops and eight potatoes before he again had the desire to speak. Achilles Daunt did not eat as much so he sat back and took the time to examine his companion.

He said, 'Pray tell me something of the land you come from, if you will. Have you seen anything of it? The land of the free, as I have heard it called.'

Dónal told him that he had indeed seen a great deal of it. He knew New England tolerably well. Had ridden over some of it. He described what he had seen of America: the whaling men out of Nantucket, the cod fisheries, the remarkable fishing schooners and catboats, the strange native boats called canoes. The country itself was magnificent, so huge that the mind could not imagine it: vast rivers and forests, the possibility of untold wealth. He had heard too of the great plains and the mountain ranges in the interior, further west.

'I have seen the redman in his own country and there is no one so fierce and so generous at once. Unless it be the people of the County Cork,' he finished with a laugh.

Achilles Daunt laughed too. 'You have had a varied life for so young a man.'

'I asked for it. I ran away to sea in '98, and I confess it was my dream to cross the ocean to America.' Dónal's face darkened. 'That was not too good neither, for to tell the truth I found myself before too long on board a Yankee slaving brig bound for the Bight of Benin, if you have ever heard of it. I do not hold with slavery, sir.'

Dónal looked carefully at Achilles Daunt. In America a statement like that in an unguarded moment might cost you a friendship – or your life.

But Achilles Daunt was nodding his head vigorously. 'It is an abomination, Mr Long. I quite agree.'

A large jug of steaming tea was placed before them and as they poured and drank Dónal gazed out the window, remembering that first cold brush with evil on the hot seas of Africa. 'What is the difference, Mr Daunt, between enslaving a black man in his native home and enslaving your neighbour in his? I will tell you. It is the colour of his skin. I have heard people say that God has ordained the white man to rule over every other race. That is way of the powerful over the weak. I notice that every man calls God to his side, but if the white man were to go into Africa without powder and shot he would soon enough learn that God does not hold with slavery.'

'You speak strongly, sir. It would be wiser not to say so much.'

'You have the right of it, Mr Daunt. But the truth is, I cannot abide the thought of it. I had a friend who, but for a stroke of fortune, would have been a slave himself. His name was Karaku, a prince of his own people. And had you seen the cruelty with which the slave trade is done, the sheer brutality and heartlessness . . . Enough of that. I will spoil your dinner, and an excellent dinner it was, too, such as I have not had since the summer of last year. For that I have you to thank.'

Achilles Daunt protested that it was small thanks for what Dónal had done. 'Is there not a single other thing I can do for you, Mr Long?'

Dónal laughed. 'Unless you can set my feet on the deck of a ship again, Mr Daunt, I fear there is not.'

Achilles Daunt was deep in thought for a while and Dónal gave his attention to the dining room. Lane's eating-house was filling up now – with captains of ships moored out in the roadstead, naval officers off duty, young fresh-faced infantry officers, businessmen, lawyers, clerks. Dónal watched them for a time before turning his attention to the window again. He saw the ships alongside the quay, the naval vessels moored beyond, the small boats plying up and down with smaller cargoes, the boatmen rowing people to their boats for a penny.

'What is that fine sloop there?' he asked, pointing to a particularly elegant boat just now working its way up channel with the tide.

'That is the *Columbine*. Mr Smith Barry's pleasure yacht that I told you about. They have got up a water club here and go about in pleasure yachts, quite in the way of old King Charles, who used to sail his ship with his own hands, I'm told. They are forever playing games and holding chases and playing at naval manoeuvres and they are assisted by Admiral Somerville and others of the navy.'

'Do you mean Captain Henry Coyle Somerville?'

'It is Admiral Somerville now. I'm glad that you know him, although he is on the West Indies Station at present. At any rate, they even race those yachts like chase-horses.'

Dónal laughed. 'I have seen the fishermen of New England racing their schooners against each other, but that was to get the fishing catch first to port so as to have the best price. And dangerous racing it was too.'

'Oh,' said Achilles Daunt airily, 'there is danger enough in our pleasure yachts.'

'Danger, sir? In a yacht? I do not believe it.'

'Indeed, young man,' said Achilles Daunt, his eyes twinkling. 'They have been fighting among themselves of late. Two of them ran foul of each other last month and they went at each other with cutlasses and handspikes. One of the masters was so vexed that on the next occasion he discharged his cannon at the other vessel. It was loaded, sir, and although the ball went high, if his aim had been truer he might have killed a sailor or two!'

The two men laughed for so long that the serving boy came over to see if they were all right. When they had recovered, Dónal said, 'But do they carry guns and cutlasses on pleasure yachts?'

'Indeed they do. For you see if they venture out they may fall foul of a French privateer or if they cruise west along the shore they must come into the territory of those blaggardly O'Driscolls who are little better than pirates. Even three or four six-pounders are sufficient to drive them away, I am told, though to be sure Mr D'Alton's pleasure yacht was lost in the region of the Kedges last year, with a crew of three and on a remarkably fine day too. Everyone believes it was O'Driscoll who sank her.'

'But surely, sir, they will not fight over so small a thing as a race, who wins or loses?'

Any man who went to sea for his bread must expect to have to fight for his life from time to time, and if he was not fighting his fellow man he would always be fighting the wind and the sea, whose immeasurable power only the sailor knows. That anyone should fight over a yacht chase was beyond Dónal's comprehension.

Achilles Daunt told him that the yachts were designed and organised like little naval vessels, armed and ready for action. That their chief sport was organising mock sea-battles 'quite like children playing with toy soldiers'. That occasionally money was laid down for a wager on which boat was the fastest, or which could sail to a certain place the soonest. That Mr Smith Barry had raced D'Alton's new boat to the Old Head of Kinsale and back on two occasions and won each time, which had vexed Mr D'Alton. That since they could never agree on any rules the yachts were perpetually running into each other, fouling each other, breaking each other's rigging and tearing sails. That their crews became so excited by the chase that they hurled objects at their worst rivals and had even been found fighting in taverns after the racing and their masters had no command of them.

'It has come to such a pitch that only last week the crew of *Althea* boarded the *Neptune* in a fit of temper, threw her captain into the sea and cut away the rigging with axes so that her mast fell down. They then repaired to their own vessel, shoved off again and went on to win the race. Although the members of the Water Club are resolved that the attack was not sporting, particularly since axes had been used, because of the lack of rules they were compelled to give the prize-money to *Althea*.

You are to consider that while the owner wins the greatest share, a considerable portion of the money is paid to the crew. They call it head-money.'

'Well,' said Dónal, 'I have fought the French and I have fought the British and in between I have fought one or two in the slaving line, but I have never fought anyone over a race. It is scarcely believable!'

Dónal and Mr Daunt parted outside Aeneas Lane's, agreeing to meet again. Dónal was anxious to get back to the fort; the sun was already in the topmasts of the ships that lay to the west of the town and his parole would be out at sunset.

'By the by,' called Achilles Daunt, as he hurried away, 'we'll see about the matter of a proper thank-you.'

6

PLEASURE YACHT RACING

The following day the colonel personally delivered a note which begged Dónal to attend at the battery at Columbine Quay at ten of the morning on the following day. There Mr Achilles Daunt would wait on him. The colonel delivered the note with a wink and a nod and said that if he heard that Dónal had gone to sea again the next day he would not turn out the guard to search for him.

'Only remember your parole,' he added, very mysteriously.

So it was that Dónal made his way down through the town on a beautiful February day – the kind that set the mind on spring and summer and the warm days ahead. Instead of the cold easterly wind, the sun came through his thin uniform and warmed his bones. His step was lighter and he whistled a cheerful tune.

As he turned to walk along the quays he was stopped by a tall thin man who drew him aside into the entrance to a lane. With much looking up and down the street and over his shoulder, the man introduced himself as a friend of America who was glad to make Dónal's acquaintance.

They shook hands and Dónal said he was glad to make the man's acquaintance, although the man had not given his name.

'Time is short, sir,' the stranger said. 'Have you anything to tell me?'

Dónal was astounded. He had never met the man before; how could he possibly have anything to say to him?

'Nothing,' he said. 'Unless, possibly, that it is a grand day?'

The man shook his head impatiently. 'You can trust me, sir.'

'I make no doubt of it, sir,' said Dónal.

'Have you heard anything at the fort? Even the merest scrap of news is grist to our mill.'

Dónal wracked his brains. What was the man talking about?

'The merest scrap of information, in the right hands, sir, can become a weapon larger than the greatest ship.'

Now it flashed upon Dónal's mind that this man was a spy. A rush of distaste and he was shrugging off the man's arm and making for the street.

'Stop, Mr Long!' the man called.

Dónal swung about. 'Why should I? I'm a fighting man, sir, not an informer.'

The man sneered. 'Is that so? You scorn the humble occupation of collector of intelligence? Oh, yes, I see it by your countenance. And you have had your trouble with informers before this, Mr Long. In 1798, I fancy.'

Dónal advanced on the stranger, his fists bunched. He seized him by the lapels and thrust him up against a gate pier. 'I hate your kind,' he said. 'I'd cut your throat for tuppence!'

The man was white-faced and stammering. 'Please. Don't hurt me, Please!'

Dónal let go again and the man squirmed from his grip. In a flash he was out of the lane and standing on the street. He turned from the safety of the crowd and called back, 'We will meet again, Mr Long. Remember '98.'

It didn't quite spoil Dónal's pleasure in the beautiful day, nor in the fact that his friend Achilles Daunt had something planned for him, but it had taken him aback to be recognised. He had thought that the events of that time, part of his boyhood, would be remembered by nobody but himself. He had not played an important role in the events of the year. Why should anyone now try to turn his actions against him?

But, Dónal remembered, this man was a spy. Spies collected information about other people. They worked on the principle that nothing was too small to be useful. No doubt this man met some sailor from his old ship, the *Leander*, or someone from his home village who knew part of the story. He would use it now to try to get Dónal to spy on the fort and collect intelligence for him. But Dónal would not abuse the good offices of the colonel who had been kind to him. At that moment the colonel's words about 'a bit of a show, something big' in the Chesapeake Bay area came into his mind. That, he told himself, was exactly the kind of news this rat of a spy would love to hear.

He came at last to Columbine Quay. The 'battery', as it had been called in Achilles Daunt's note, was just a rusty old carronade on a truckle. Dónal thought it would hardly be powerful enough to lob a stone into the water at this stage, not to mind a heavy shot. He was peering down the barrel to see if the inside was rusty too when a shout of 'Mr Long, ahoy!' made him whirl round.

It was Achilles Daunt standing on the deck of a fine pleasure yacht tied up alongside the quay. 'Good morning to you, Mr Long. Will you come aboard the *Iliad*?'

Dónal's jaws fell open. The yacht was a fine cutter, not dressed up or ornamented as the other boats around. No fine flags or gold leaf paint. No decorative brass bells or cushions on the seats. It was a trim, well maintained cutter of the type that any naval officer would approve. Dónal stepped aboard it with something approaching joy.

'Is this what your note was for?' he asked, beaming about him.

'It is,' said Achilles Daunt. 'And a bit more besides. Come below now, I want you to meet my crew. We're going to watch the racing.'

Below decks the yacht was truly beautiful. Brass lamps swung in gimbals that kept them level even when the boat was tilted over by the wind, there were leather benches along the side, polished timber everywhere, and joy of joys, a stove with a roaring fire throwing heat all round. But most surprising of all, the 'crew', as Achilles Daunt called them, was a young boy of perhaps ten years, introduced as 'Thomas Daunt, my youngest grandson', a young girl of about fourteen, 'Alice Daunt, my youngest granddaughter' and finally a young woman of nineteen or twenty. 'This,' said Achilles Daunt, 'is Ellen Daunt, my granddaughter, first mate of this vessel. May I introduce

Lieutenant Dónal Long, late of the schooner *Shenendoah?*'

She was almost as tall as himself, Dónal noted, with fine and regular features. Her hair was piled back on her head in the fashion of the time, but well tied down lest it blow away in the sailing wind. She wore a dress of some coarse material which did not show her figure off to advantage. But just the same, Dónal concluded, she was a beauty.

She shook his hand with an amused smile and welcomed him aboard, but Dónal thought he detected an edge to her voice and he was proved right by her next remark. 'I am not familiar with the question of military rank, sir,' she said. 'But I hope the fact that I am first mate here will not prevent you giving us the benefit of your vast practical knowledge.'

'I am sure I could not add to your knowledge, Miss Daunt,' Dónal said, a little taken aback by her attitude. 'My experience has been entirely in large vessels.'

'Oh we count ourselves a large vessel too, Mr Long. In yachting circles the *Iliad* is regarded as well-found and practical, as well as large enough to accommodate her crew. And of course, here, we do not have the assistance of a hundred sailors who can be driven along with a blow of a rope's end or the threat of hanging. On this ship we must all work.'

'You are quite well informed of naval practice, Miss Daunt. I look forward to seeing your handling of the yacht. It should be instructive.'

Achilles Daunt had been watching this conversation with a mischievous sparkle in his eye. 'I see you will get along famously,' he said. 'Now all hands to unmoor.'

Dónal was, in fact, very favourably impressed by the

way the little crew slipped the lines and brought the yacht out into open water. Then the tide and the slight breeze carried them down past the old town, past the line of taverns that people called 'the Holy Ground' and down past the Spithead. From the deck he could see the fort at Carrignafoy. He even fancied he could see Captain Veasey pacing up and down the barrack square in the sunshine.

A breeze was coming up now and the *Iliad* heeled to it. Dónal watched as Thomas and Alice handled the headsail sheets. Achilles himself had the tiller, while Ellen controlled the big mainsail.

Soon they were ghosting up to anchor beyond the Spithead. He had time to notice the arrival of the Water Club fleet, a majestically flagged ship at its head.

'Oh, that is Lord Inchiquin,' said Ellen, dismissively. 'He is our admiral.'

'He is so old,' said Thomas. 'Too old to be an admiral, don't you think, Lieutenant?'

Dónal laughed. 'I fear, master Thomas, that admirals are almost all too old. And very silly at times, too. It is almost a part of the job.'

Thomas thought this was really amusing and related the joke to Alice several times during the day. Ellen, on the other hand, pretended she did not hear it and set about naming the various yachts as they came abreast.

'That is Mr Smith Barry's *Columbine*. And Mr Fitzgerald's *Winsome*. What a comical name for a pleasure yacht . . . '

Eleven pleasure yachts of assorted sizes came to anchor off the Spithead. All the crews were in a high state of excitement. This was the first race of the season, Achilles Daunt told Dónal, and every sailor would get some kind of bonus for winning. The yachts were watched from the shore and from a variety of smaller craft by the gentlemen of the Water Club and their ladies: gentlemen never raced their own boats, of course, any more than they would have ridden their own horses in the horse racing. Unless, that is, they were Achilles Daunt. Most stood by with telescopes and picnic baskets, their servants shading them with parasols from the unseasonal sun.

The guns were fired and the yachts were away, and it seemed to Dónal, long used to the more exciting chases of wartime, that this race was dull stuff indeed. It seemed to go on for ever, but when at last the yachts came within sight of the finishing line, Achilles Daunt brought forth a large basket of food. They dined upon it in style, sitting on deck and watching the yachtsmen exerting themselves to pass the line before the breeze turned and blew in their faces. Dónal was overjoyed to see slices of cold tongue, great chunks of bread and butter, cold potatoes in cream, fruit and cheese. He complimented Ellen on her cooking, only to be told coldly that 'it did not take a great cook to boil potatoes'.

Dónal was hurt by her coldness. 'I am sure, Miss Daunt, cold potatoes are of little consequence to a young lady who has her own home to go to. But I assure you they are better than gold and silver to one who has spent the last month in prison.'

He could see that his speech had an effect on her because her cheeks kindled and she made an effort to be nice to him after that.

Later in the day they took the *Iliad* out for a run. Dónal

sat back and allowed himself to be sailed for a change. He was agreeably surprised at Ellen's skill when they hit the larger waves at the mouth of the harbour. She tacked the boat beautifully through one particularly rough patch. It had simply never occurred to him before now that girls might be able to sail boats as well as boys. He had spent almost all his life in the company of men and had come to think that women and girls were simply not made for a life of adventure. He would have to give more thought to the idea. When they turned the boat's head for home he was more than a little disappointed.

Achilles Daunt was proud of his grandchildren. He explained to Dónal that their parents had died in an outbreak of typhoid in the city and that he, Achilles Daunt, was now their sole protector. He smiled whenever Dónal praised them and repeatedly pointed out their abilities. 'Why, they can even lay and fire a gun, at least Ellen can,' he said.

There were two light cannon on each side, peashooters by comparison with the ones Dónal was used to.

'I did not think such guns could be used,' Dónal said. 'I supposed they were entirely for show.'

'No indeed,' replied Achilles Daunt. 'It might well happen that we need them for defence. I have taught all my crew to serve them. Ellen can lay a gun as well as any gun captain in a ship of the line.'

Privately, Dónal thought that Achilles Daunt was exaggerating the abilities of his grandchildren. Who ever heard of a girl who could shoot!

They parted with Ellen, and Alice and Thomas went to find a friend who had been on one of the other yachts. Achilles Daunt had explained to Dónal that there would be 'a little party' at the Water Club's rooms and he had promised to bring Dónal to it. 'They all want to meet the first officer of the *Shenendoah*.'

'I can hardly believe that,' Dónal said. 'She was not a ship of the line or even a frigate, you know.'

'Oh, but the action you fought with the *Lion* is quite famous. Lieutenant Congreve has described it to us in detail.'

And so Dónal found himself almost the guest of honour at the Water Club's first gathering of the season. The race had, apparently, been a great success for some. Mr Uniacke Fitzgerald had won a hundred pounds and 'a fine fast horse from his friends' and was celebrating in style. Claret flowed and food was plentiful. Dónal was the centre of many enquiries. He was pressed for a description of the battle and several times he heard the words 'just as Congreve said it was' or 'Congreve was right'. When he described the arrival of the line squall that had ruined them they sympathised and then wanted to know all about line squalls 'which we do not see in these waters, as you know, sir.'

Then they wanted to know his life story. He had to tell the tale of how he had left Ireland, how he had fought in the *Leander* when she attacked the French frigate, his subsequent days on the slaving brig and his Atlantic crossing. He did not tell them of how he had been imprisoned as a rebel in '98, nor how he had escaped with the help of his sailor friends. The conversation turned to commerce and they wondered if they could buy in some of the American schooners. Did he think Ireland might have such ships? How did he find Ireland after being away so long.

Here Dónal grew serious. 'I cannot say I see prosperity

here; indeed it seems to me that the country is much cast down of late. I except the town of Cove, of course, which thrives as far as I can see. But as I walk along the quayside every day – I have been given my parole as you know, gentlemen – I find the beggared and the destitute on every side. The small farmer is ruined. The weaver finds no work in his trade. The emigrant boat is overflowing; so many young men and women take ship for America that I fear there will be no one left for the next generation.'

It was the closest thing to a political statement Dónal had made since he was a boy. He wondered at himself. What had driven him to this? Surely the poverty of Ireland was nothing to him – he who would take ship for the Chesapeake on the first day of peace? Surely the sufferings of the small farmers of Ireland under the Act of Union could not make the slightest difference to him? He had abandoned his father's United Irishman principles the day he got his mate's ticket, declaring to himself that he would follow nothing but his own interests in future, and that he would make his new life in the New World.

There was a little murmur of disagreement at Dónal's words, as though he had offended people, but one young man nodded his head violently. 'It is the late Act. The Act of Union,' he said. 'It has been the ruin of trade. Since parliament was abolished nothing has prospered. They tax our trade to the extreme.'

'That is young Lane,' Achilles Daunt told him. 'He is very advanced in his politics. Something of a firebrand.'

'For shame,' said Mr Smith Barry. ''Tis a confounded disloyalty to say such a thing. The Union is our best hope. We must cleave to England and put our trust in the King.'

A chorus of approval. 'God save the king!' 'Long live the king!'

Lane winked at Dónal and cried 'Erin go brách!' and a shocked silence followed. An old gentlemen who had been smiling broadly on everyone suddenly upset his glass of spirits on his neighbour and cried out that 'the man was a veritable Bonapartist!'

The situation was saved by Mr Uniacke Fitzgerald. 'I believe we have resolved that no politics will be talked in the Water Club.'

Someone said that wishing health to the king was not politics but loyalty and Mr Lane replied that wishing well to Ireland could hardly be called disloyal.

A fresh-faced young man in the club's full dress uniform announced that he would now sing one of the melodies of Mr Moore, and Mr Uniacke Fitzgerald said that it was appropriate since Mr Moore, who was an admiralty registrar in Bermuda, was something in the seafaring line himself. The young man began to sing in a sweet baritone, 'The Harp that Once Through Tara's Halls'.

'That is young Murrough O'Bryen,' Achilles Daunt said, 'second son of Lord Inchiquin. When he starts to sing there be no stopping him up. Lord Inchiquin is our Admiral, you know.'

Achilles Daunt drew Dónal into a quiet corner where another gentleman, almost as old as Daunt, began to question him about the rigging of the *Shenendoah* – a subject which seemed to fascinate everyone at the Water Club. They moved on from there to the general rigging of ships, the windward performance of schooners and other fore-and-aft rigged vessels, the horrible danger of a lee shore, especially for square-rigged ships, the great advantage of an Atlantic crossing in the trade winds, the painful effects of scurvy and countless other fascinating subjects.

As Dónal made his way back up the hill towards the fort that evening his heart was light, his head spinning from the effects of too much claret. The Water Club had been most hospitable, he told himself. He had been made to feel quite at home. It had been a tremendous day – fresh sea air, good food, delightful company – even if it was a bit irritating that Ellen Daunt had taken so obvious a dislike to him.

On his way past the spot where he had met the American spy that morning, he began to have the impression that he was being followed. He turned suddenly and was in time to see a lame old man go in the door of a tavern in a hurry. It was not the sight of the man that shook him; sailors, lame or otherwise, came and went all day. What startled him was the fact that he was certain he knew the man, though he could not name him at that moment. And now that he thought about it, he could remember hearing that lame step ever since he left Columbine Quay. He was about to turn back and go into the tavern when he remembered that it was already close to sunset and he must not break his parole. He hurried on towards the fort, his mind full of that mysterious man and the American spy.

7

MISS DAUNT

Apparently there had been a party at Admiralty House and a discussion had arisen as to the sailing abilities of the American and British Navies. And, it seemed, Lieutenant Congreve had offended some ancient captain or admiral by describing the handling of the *Shenendoah* as 'the finest piece of seamanship he had ever seen'. Then Achilles Daunt had thrown in his word, and one word borrowed another until it seemed that the honour of the Empire was at stake. At which point the gentlemen of the Water Club, the officers of the navy and certain men of importance in the town, had laid their money down on a race between America and Britain.

The Colonel had been summoned and ordered to furnish the prisoner Dónal Long to sail the pleasure yacht of his choice in a duel against the chosen yacht of the Admiralty. That was what had Dónal anxiously pacing the deck of the *Iliad* now and watching Lieutenant Congreve pacing the deck of *Columbine* not far away.

At first when Achilles Daunt had informed Dónal of the bet he had laughed and said he knew nothing of pleasure yacht racing. Then, imagining the feel of the deck under his feet again, the roll of the waves, the salt wind on his face, he had said he would do it. Next, he had foolishly said he could want no better ship than Achilles Daunt's own yacht, which had delighted the old man.

'By God, sir,' he laughed. 'You shall have your pick of the yacht crews in this harbour. I shall pay for them myself! To think of the old *Iliad* racing under the command of a privateersman!'

Dónal thought of the day Achilles Daunt had taken him out. 'Why, sir, surely there is no one so well versed in the behaviour of your yacht as your own crew?' If Achilles Daunt agreed to that, Dónal imagined that he would teach that saucy Ellen Daunt a thing or two about sailing. She had been cold and contemptuous towards him because he was a mere passenger. Now he would be captain and she would be mate. She would have to obey *his* orders. He would enjoy his revenge.

'By God, sir, I believe you have the right of it. Ain't this the spectacle!' Achilles Daunt rubbed his hands with glee and the whole thing was settled.

Now he regretted it. The *Iliad* rode at anchor in a rising gale. It was the first day of March, and the month was keeping its old promise to 'come in like a lion'. The swells rushed in from the harbour entrance, funnelled between the two headlands that narrowed the harbour, and then charged at the Spithead to make the yachts plunge up and down continually. Twenty yards away the *Columbine* was plunging too, and Dónal noted that every once in a while her bow plunged into a swell and shook green water over her decks. Congreve was anxiously pacing the deck, one eye on the crew and another on the admiral's yacht, from which the gun would be fired that would signal the beginning of the race.

Dónal looked around him at his crew, Ellen, Alice and Thomas, not one of them heavy enough to raise the anchor in this sea. He would have to do it himself. He thought quickly. He would guess that Congreve was very much aware that he was sailing Mr Smith Barry's yacht, and very conscious that this same gentleman held great influence. If Congreve were to damage the yacht at the very starting line, under the eyes of her owner, he might never get promotion. That gave Dónal the advantage. He would sail right across in front of the *Columbine* and force her to give way. It was a nasty trick but by all accounts this yacht racing was not so different from fighting.

He called Ellen. 'Miss Daunt,' he said, 'I would be grateful if you would lay her on a larboard tack as soon as I break the anchor out. Please instruct Thomas and Alice to raise the headsails.' He was pleased to see Ellen Daunt swallow a cutting reply and say 'Aye aye' instead, like any good seaman.

She took the tiller and he went forward and began to haul in the anchor cable. Out of the corner of his eye he saw two burly men doing the same on the *Columbine*.

Then the gun went off on the admiral's yacht and Dónal was hauling hand over hand so fast that he thought his arms would pull from their sockets. The wet rope was coming in, though, and he used the motion of the waves to help him. At one point he was enveloped in a cloud of canvas as the staysail went up, but he carried on hauling. At last he felt the anchor break free of the Spithead mud and he shouted, with what breath he had left. 'Anchor's aweigh!'

Before he had properly stowed the anchor he felt the decks tilt and knew that Ellen had done as he ordered. He shouted for Thomas to stow the anchor properly and went aft to stand by the tiller.

'Steady,' he said. Congreve had got the *Columbine* going somewhat earlier but because of the direction of the wind they were slightly behind the *Iliad*.

'We'll cross her bows,' Dónal shouted, the fire of battle in his veins.

'We will not, Mr Long,' she replied. 'We will strike her in the bows.'

Dónal bit back his reply. He had been an officer now for too long. Had a sailor in any of his ships replied like that he would have received a flogging. It was the next thing to mutiny to question an officer's orders. However, this was Miss Daunt, not some second lieutenant or master's mate. She was the owner's granddaughter.

'Keep her steady, Miss Daunt,' he said, calmly.

He watched as the *Columbine* came towards them, gathering speed as she came. She had a wicked long bowsprit that stuck out in front and would tear the *Iliad's* rigging to bits if they struck. He could see Congreve's face quite clearly, and he watched as shock, then horror swept over it as it dawned on him that Dónal was not going to turn, that he was going to keep going and risk a crash.

Would Congreve give way? That was the question. Seconds passed. A minute. The boats drew closer. Now they were separated by no more than a couple of boat-lengths. It was the critical moment. Then Dónal saw a nervous movement of Congreve's head. It was as if the lieutenant were looking over his shoulder at the spectators gathered on the deck of the admiral's yacht. Mr Smith Barry would be there, watching anxiously as his pride and joy went straight to her destruction.

Dónal saw Congreve give the order and the seamen spring to their sheets. The Columbine's head swung up into the wind, but the movement was badly timed. The jib was caught aback. The *Columbine* stopped dead to the wind, bobbing up and down twenty feet away as the *Iliad* slipped past.

'She missed stays!' Dónal gasped. 'We did it.' He looked at Ellen Daunt but she was frowning.

'That was not a sporting thing to do,' she said haughtily.

'Madam,' said Dónal, with ice in his voice, 'perhaps you would direct your attention to your brother. He is attempting to set the topsail and making a poor hand of it.' She turned away abruptly and went forward to help Thomas.

With the topsail set, the *Iliad* heeled steeply so that her lee rail was under water at times and water foamed along her side. Thomas and Alice came stumbling back, their faces glowing, their eyes shining, passing remarks to each other about the 'tremendous speed that the old cutter could do'. Ellen stayed forward, one hand round the mast, the other clenched in a tight fist at her side. She had not wanted to come on this race but her grandfather had insisted. Who else knew the boat as well as she, he had said. The young American would need her advice and guidance. She had been flattered into coming and now she regretted it. The young man did not need her advice; far from it. He was as arrogant as all Americans were supposed to be, and would not listen to anything she said. Worse than that, she knew he had guessed correctly what

Congreve would do and that her remark about unsporting behaviour had been wrong. There was nothing either in the letter of the rules or their spirit that would prohibit Dónal Long from doing what he did.

Dónal soon had the *Iliad* over on the other tack, her bowsprit pointed straight down the harbour. The mark they had to round – it would be a barrel, bobbing up and down on the sea, almost invisible from the deck of a warship not to mind a yacht – was five miles to leeward near Poer Head. Once round that they would have to beat up to wind again, the waves and the wind forcing them backwards and sideways so that the rocky shore would be a great danger. The wind was rising too. Already he could feel that the yacht was overpressed. He would have to take in the topsail and possibly the flying jib.

Columbine was moving again. She plunged and reared through the waves, every stitch of canvas set in an effort to catch up. There would be no tricks now. The rest of the race would be pure seamanship. The *Iliad* had gained a slight lead but once they had rounded the mark and were facing the long Atlantic swells, the *Columbine's* greater weight would give her an advantage.

They were past the lighthouse now and Dónal was swinging downwind on a course that would clear the notorious Cow and Calf rocks.

It was an hour's run to the mark and in that time Dónal had taken in the topsail and flying jib, and put a reef in the mainsail. He was keenly aware that the wind had risen greatly. When he looked back into the eye of the wind there was white water everywhere and now he could see a squall coming down towards them, a cloud blacker than the rest and the sheets of rain curtaining the far shore. The wind had veered too and was now coming slightly north of west. It made him think of that terrible line-squall that had battered the *Shenendoah*.

They should have called the race off, he now felt. Or he himself should have withdrawn, not because he feared for his ship or his own life but because he was racing the yacht with a crew of children. His heart was sick with terror and remorse. For his own pride and the pleasure of sailing he had endangered these young people. It was not an officer-like thing to do.

Thomas was seasick, pale, almost green, vomiting into a canvas bucket. Alice was only slightly better but she was still taking an interest in the race. Ellen, stony-faced, huddled in a corner of the windward rail, her feet braced against a piece of the coaming.

Columbine was coming up fast behind them, still carrying a full mainsail and staysail and jib. With a complete crew she could still race in the wind.

Dónal handed the tiller to Alice and told her to keep the course as steady as she could. He knelt beside Ellen. 'This is getting very bad,' he said. She nodded agreement. 'I'm going to bring her head to wind and lie to until that squall is past. I'm afraid we'll be out of the race.'

She looked up at him scornfully. 'You are the captain,' she told him. 'Do not ask me to make your decisions. It is your responsibility.'

Dónal deserved that, he knew. He had enjoyed proving her wrong earlier. Now he was paying for it.

Ten minutes later the squall was on them. Had they been

still racing they would have broached to in the howling wind, perhaps capsized or lost the mast. Instead, the *Iliad* lay hove to, wallowing against the gale. She had only a scrap of sail on the mainmast and the tiny staysail, yet she was heeled over so much that Dónal was up to his ankles in water as he braced himself at the tiller. He had sent the others below where they could stay warm and dry.

In time the squall cleared but amazingly the wind hardly went down at all. The clouds too had become lower and now Dónal was surrounded by a fine mist that drove into his face and found its way down the his neck and up his sleeves. *Columbine* was gone, cut off from his sight. He could not see Poer Head, though he knew by the feel of the sea that it could not be far away. Neither could he see the shore.

There was no question now of working back against this wind. The gale had risen to such a pitch that any seaman would know his duty: to run off before the gale, to keep away from the dangerous shore that was under his lee. At times like this, sailors talked of 'sea-room', the need to put as much space between the ship and the land as possible. Out there on the deep he would take in all sail and let the boat wash around on the waves like a cork. She would be perfectly safe, although it would be uncomfortable. In here, with the high cliffs of Poer Head an unknown distance away in the mist, he was in the greatest possible danger.

There was nothing for it. Dónal put the helm over and felt the *Iliad* gather way. As she did he leant forward and freed the mainsheet so that the sail could draw properly. The boat came slightly more upright and then she was off, coursing over the waves. Sometimes she kept pace with a wave for a while, the white water running on either side. At other times Dónal would hear a hiss and a roar behind him and turn in time to see a huge breaker rising above the *Iliad*'s stern. He would turn the boat a little then, taking the wave on the quarter. Incredibly, none of them dropped on to the boat. The *Iliad* kept her head for hours, rushing away south-eastward, running with the gale.

In that time, through his growing exhaustion, Dónal came to respect the little boat. The shipwrights who had made her (in the village of Crosshaven he had been told) had done their work well. The man who laid out her lines made sure that she could weather almost anything the sea could throw at her. All through that afternoon and the night she looked after him. The sea threw its might at him, the worst it could do. The wind screamed in the rigging like a banshee. His breath was torn out of him by the force of it. He felt himself battered by an icy hand. But *Iliad*'s stern rose to the following seas, her bow plunged and threw off the water like a dog shaking herself. When she heeled in the gusts she put her lee rail under but he never felt that sickening dread that *this* time she might not come back. He never felt the dead weight in the tiller that told him that she would not steer, nor did he have to struggle with the arm-wrenching power of a tiller that could not hold the boat before the wind. The *Iliad* inspired only confidence. When Ellen Daunt came on deck he felt as if he had been steering for days, not hours, as if he had careered across the face of the earth instead of through twenty or thirty miles of broken sea. But he was not weary of it: he was jubilant though tired.

'This is a mighty fine ship,' Dónal said, grinning from ear to ear. His humour infected Ellen so that her icy coldness dissolved and she smiled too. She took her place beside him at the tiller, a ridiculous bundle of clothes, tarry jackets, men's breeches, sea-boots, the whole thing topped by a battered tarpaulin hat that a fisherman would be ashamed of. 'I'll take her for a time, Mr Long,' she said, and he cheerfully left the tiller to her.

The next five minutes Dónal spent trying to get the feeling back in his icy hands. It was March, and out here it was still winter. Although Ellen had passed a warm fearnought jacket up to him earlier it had not kept the spray or the cold out. He flapped his hands against his sides and opened and closed the fists. He worked his toes in his soggy leather boots. He rubbed his nose with the flat of his hand to get the icy tip to come to life again. Then Alice was passing a warm drink up to him. It was tea. Had the sea settled to the point where they could light the stove? Sure enough, smoke was puffing from the chimney and blowing away instantly in the wind.

Now that he looked around him he saw that the sea was not so rough. A scrap of moon had broken through the clouds and the wind was not screaming in the rigging so much. It looked like they had weathered the gale.

He looked at Ellen and for the first time their eyes met. She was smiling.

'It is a wild night,' she said.

'Indeed it is, Miss Daunt,' he replied.

'You have managed splendidly,' she said, her eyes shining. 'Quite splendidly.' She still had to shout the words.

'Thank you, Miss Daunt,' Dónal replied, suddenly proud of himself. 'But it is no more than any seaman would do.'

'Nevertheless . . . ' she shouted, but she never finished the sentence because a particularly nasty wave threw cold water on both of them.

They hurtled on through the night, crashing from the tops of waves and wallowing in the troughs. They took turns at steering until the cold grey dawn showed that at last the storm was passing. Far to the east Dónal could see an edge to the clouds, patches of lighter grey, and as the sun rose, he could even see blue sky. 'I think we might get a little more sail on, Miss Daunt,' he said.

But Miss Daunt was fast asleep, sprawled against the companionway doors, her feet braced inelegantly against the coamings, the tarpaulin hat raked back off her face by the force of the wind. Dónal realised with a start, for the second time, that the face under the hat was beautiful. Ellen's long lashes lay on her cheeks like threads of silk. Her lips were curled almost into a smile. Her cheeks, reddened by the wind, looked for all the world like ripe apples. There was something in the turn of her nose and the firmness of her chin that made him want to touch them. It was with difficulty that he took his eyes from her and turned his attention to the pressing worry of how to round up into the wind, a manoeuvre that involved turning across the seas in such a way that the boat might easily be capsized. This problem, nevertheless, was not sufficiently consuming to keep him from glancing frequently at the face that reposed beneath the unflattering tarpaulin hat.

8

ENEMY IN SIGHT

As so often happens at sea, once the gale had blown itself
out the day was clear, the sky an intense blue. The wind
blew fitfully, occasionally becoming strong and bringing
a touch of winter with it. But as the day wore on, the sea
calmed and the breeze settled into the southwest. It was
a good wind for the long sail home, a 'soldier's wind' as
sailors called it. It would have been perfect except that
the wind became lighter and lighter as the day went on,
until by late afternoon the *Iliad* was barely moving over
the sea.

Thomas and Alice had stationed themselves forward
of the mast and, wrapped in their coats, were soaking up
the sunshine. Ellen and Dónal sat by the tiller, talking.
Ellen was worried about what her grandfather would think.

'He will fear us wrecked in the gale. He will have
people out scouring the cliffs. Alas, my poor grandfather.'

Dónal reassured her that her grandfather knew the
boat, knew she was capable of weathering the gale. He was
a better seaman than to fear the worst at every flaw of
wind. But in his heart he knew Ellen was right. And to her

fear was added another of his own: the colonel would believe he had escaped. He would think that Dónal had broken his solemn word of honour, dishonoured his parole and run for America, taking the children and Ellen with him, perhaps as hostages. It was an unbearable thought.

There was nothing he could do just then. They had spread every stitch of sail the *Iliad* could carry – the big brown mainsail, the jackyard topsail above that; the staysail, jib and flying jib. There was a tiny trysail that Dónal had spread beneath the boom, a little like a watersail in a big ship, but he could see that it would not draw and had taken it in again. He could make no further effort, and the afternoon was wearing on into dark. Before the light went, he knew, he would have to reduce that sail. If a squall came on them in the darkness he could not depend on the strength of his crew. He would have to play for safety with less sail, and that would slow the boat even more.

There was a little food in the galley – some bread and hard-boiled eggs, some cold ham and biscuits. This was considered sufficient to feed the tiny crew for the day of the race. Ellen had wisely rationed the supplies once the storm came so that, although they were not 'fed like turkey-cocks' as she said, neither were they hungry. They would do for another night and day. Dónal wondered if they should fish, but not knowing whether *Iliad* carried any hooks he decided to postpone making any decision about it.

Sometime during those long hours Dónal found courage to ask Ellen about the death of her parents. He pointed out the coincidence that both he and she had lost their parents to the fever and she told him of her great grief when her mother and father died, and of her continuing sense of loss. Then she made him tell the story of his life, and he told it in bits and pieces, always underplaying his own part in things: how he had run away from home as a child; how he had been in action against the *Indomptable;* how his friend Charlie Madden had died; how he had voyaged in the detestable slave-ship; how they had fought the Barbary pirates. He recounted how he had escaped from the slaver and made his way to America. His time in the New World, working his way up to the rank of first officer seemed dull by comparison, but she was full of questions of a most seamanlike nature, the kind of sensible questions that he would never have expected from a girl. She wanted to know about the curious rigs of the New England catboats, the extreme rake of a schooner's masts, their speed, their usefulness in trade. Then when he came to the war of 1812 she listened as he told how he had come to join the privateer, the tales of their fights in the bay of Mexico, their captures, the actions they had fought and lost. At last he came to the battle with Lieutenant Congreve's brig. She heartily approved of the *Shenendoah.*

'It is a heroic tale,' she said, as darkness settled around them once again. 'That one man so young should have had so many adventures and lived to tell the tale. I declare, it is like something out of a play or a Greek legend.'

Dónal had no time to bask in her admiration. The breeze was freshening again and he had to take in the extra sails and reef the main. While that was being done Ellen was below decks and shortly she passed up a lump of bread and butter and a slice of ham. Warm tea followed it. Dónal did not realise he was hungry, but when the food came he wolfed it down like a man who had starved for weeks. Then he settled down to navigate by the fitful stars.

They worked the night-watch by watch, four hours on and four hours off. Dónal kept his watch alone, but when Ellen was on watch he made sure that one of the other young people accompanied her. He slept in the pilot-berth, a little bed that was close to the hatch so that he could come on deck quickly if required. But all went well and in the watery dawn they were rewarded by the thinnest line of grey along the horizon. It was the coast of Ireland again.

Unaccountably, the wind became light with the dawn and once again they crept painfully slowly towards the land. As the morning drew on, the sky filled with those wisps of cloud that sailor's call mares' tails. Dónal taught Thomas and Alice the rhyme:

> Mackerel skies and mares' tails
> Make lofty ships carry low sails.

Those beautiful wisps were the sign of a coming wind. Before long they would be battling the sea again, and already the swell was increasing from the southwest, the forerunner of the storm. But this time they were not downcast. Every hour showed the land more clearly. There was just the chance that they would reach harbour before the worst of it came on them.

The rain came first, a fine drizzle that dimpled the smooth sea. Then the wind came and the drizzle thickened. Soon the *Iliad* was surging along under staysail and reefed main. It was exhilarating, and Thomas and Alice laughed as she threw water aside and forged across the wave-tops.

At about three o'clock in the afternoon they sighted the lighthouse of Roches Point. Two or three hours now and they would be home. They would escape the worst of the storm.

The next minute Thomas shouted 'A sail! A sail!' and Dónal, looking where he pointed, saw the sails of a man o'war emerge from a heavier patch of rain almost between the *Iliad* and the harbour. The others were jabbering with delight, Thomas even leaping up and down, but Dónal was studying her and he knew by her bluff bow and the cut of her sails that she was French.

'Silence fore and aft,' he shouted, thinking in his concentration that he was back aboard his schooner again, and the fierce authority of his voice quietened everyone, including Ellen. She looked up at him with big shocked eyes but said nothing.

'Hands to the sheets,' he said. 'What armament have we, Miss Daunt?'

'But . . . '

'That is a French vessel, Miss Daunt. She will try to take us.'

Ellen gulped. She was about to say something else but a look from Dónal silenced her before she could begin. She thought quickly and remembered the two small cannon on each side of the yacht. She reported this and Dónal told her to take the tiller and hold the course.

He brought Thomas below with him and in five minutes had manhandled the four tiny popguns on to the deck. None of them was powerful enough to make even the tiniest hole in the French ship's side, but Dónal was determined to put up some sort of fight. A French ship would take delight in snapping up a gentleman's yacht. The captain would be proud to keep her for himself and sail it round the harbour of Brest or wherever he was stationed. Dónal would do his best to return the *Iliad* to Achilles Daunt but he was going to annoy the French in the process.

He set up and charged the guns. 'Can you use these?' he asked Thomas, and the boy nodded his head. 'Grandfather made us all learn.' The boy's hands shook, but Dónal saw that he would do what he was told. 'You're a fighting lad,' he told him. 'A brave lad. I should be glad to serve with you in any ship, and you too, Alice.'

The *Iliad* was moving briskly. The French ship was moving even faster. In a matter of minutes she had closed off the entrance to the harbour and was bracing her yardarms round so that she could come down on the *Iliad*. She was broad on the wind – the best point of sail for a ship like that.

The *Iliad's* best point of sail, the point by which he could easiest outrun the Frenchman, was into the eye of the wind, or as close to it as she would go. She was like a schooner in that, and Dónal knew schooners like the back of his hand. No man o'war could follow her there. But that course would take her into the arms of the enemy. If he stood in for the coast and safety, Dónal knew they would have to pass under the guns of the oncoming ship. On the other hand he could not turn and run, for the big ship would soon catch him up. In the end, he felt he had no choice. They would run at the Frenchman and see what would come of it. He did not think so big a ship would fire on a pleasure-yacht full of children.

Dónal studied the ship carefully. What was her course? His practised eye told him that if he went about now and pointed as close to the wind as ever the *Iliad* would go he would cross the enemy's bow. Certainly they would have bow-chasers, guns mounted in the front of the ship. Perhaps they would fire on him, or near him, and perhaps the *Iliad* might return fire. However they would not be likely to hit him and they would not be likely to get off more than a shot or two. The more he examined the path of the enemy ship the more he became convinced that this was the only course open to him.

'All hands to tack ship.' The children stared at him. Their faces showed fear as clearly as Dónal had ever seen it, but they hesitated for only a moment. Then they leapt to their stations and prepared to tack.

'Helm's a-lee,' Dónal shouted. The wind had risen now and as the *Iliad* came round into it, and the noise in the rigging rose, it occurred to Dónal that he had picked a bad week to commence his yacht-racing career.

'I do believe you are going to attack her,' Ellen said. 'I commend you for it. It is a brave thing.'

Dónal was thinking that Ellen herself was brave enough, standing there on the deck with the prospect of death in a hail of cannon balls coming closer by the minute.

The *Iliad* was foaming along now, strake after strake going under, until water streamed over the deck and the lee cannons dipped their stoppered mouths every time a gust caught her. Ellen said she was worried, not just because they were racing directly towards the enemy, but because the ship was overpressed.

Dónal agreed but declared they could not spare the time to reef. 'We must keep on, Ellen. Our lives depend on it. We may cross her course far enough away to avoid taking a shot.'

Twilight set in far earlier than expected. The *Iliad* and the enemy ship raced towards each other in the gloom, a gloom that made the big ship's sails stand out like lamps against the cloud. At one point she fired a gun and a signal ran up her mast. At the distance Dónal could not read it, but he was certain of what it said: *Heave to*, with the possible addition of *or we will sink you*. He had seen such signals before. He was not going to give his ship away without a fight.

Now the red ensign of Great Britain broke out at the mast but Dónal explained to Ellen and the others that this was a trick. She would lower the flag just before going into action and run up the French one instead. Her captain no doubt believed that Dónal would see the flag and heave to. Once the French ship was within range *Iliad* would be at her mercy. 'I know a trick worth two of that,' he told them. 'Thomas, have we any signal flags?' When Thomas nodded that they had Dónal told him to 'bring up a blast of signal flags and run them up any old way.' The signals were brought from the flag locker in the tiny fore cabin and Thomas asked what he should run up. Dónal thought for a moment.

'Run up signal flag U. That means,' he told the others, '*You are standing into danger*. That should amuse them. Do you not think it will amuse them, Miss Daunt?' Ellen nodded eagerly.

But Dónal was becoming more and more worried. The little *Iliad* ran on, closing on the massive shape of the enemy ship, but it did not seem to Dónal that she ran as fast as before. Their courses were drawing together. The

Iliad would not pass far ahead of the enemy ship but close under her bow, and once she had run past the bow and cleared the bowchasers she would be exposed to the full force of the broadside – three decks of guns all firing at once. The little yacht would simply crumble. If the French captain chose to destroy them, Dónal would have brought his friend's grandchildren to certain death. How could he be certain that the Frenchman would care about the children of an enemy nation?

What should he do?

There was one chance now, and that was a slim one. The French expected him to hold his course, to pass under their bow. Once he had passed them on that side they could not follow him, they knew that. They knew too that if he ran clear on he would escape and make Cove and their presence would be reported. 'If I was on board that ship,' he told himself, 'I guess I would concentrate all my best men on the starboard guns. I might not even have the larboard guns manned if I was any way short of men. If I can tack almost under her bows I might be able to pass her on that larboard side. I might catch them unawares.'

The problems were threefold. Firstly he would have to pass those bow-chasers. One of them might hole a sail or blow the mast away. Secondly the *Iliad* might miss stays and just sit there in the water, in which case the hundreds of tons of oak and iron that was the enemy ship would simply roll over her as a carriage-wheel might roll over a snail. The crew might not even notice the collision. Even if they escaped that fate, he would lose the wind as he passed down the larboard side. The mainsail and headsails were set too low to catch any wind across the big man o'war. Still it was his best chance.

'All hands stand by to tack ship,' Dónal ordered. 'Ellen come aft.' He explained the situation to her. 'Now what I want to do is to have the topsail ready. As soon as we tack I want it run up. It might be high enough to catch the wind and keep us moving. and by the way, clear the larboard guns for action. And do it secretly, I don't want those Frenchies seeing it.'

In five minutes the topsail was ready to go up and the larboard guns were ready. In ten minutes they were within range of the bow-chasers. The red ensign still flew at the man o'war's truck but at that moment a puff of smoke on her bow told them that the battle had commenced. At the same time the flag came rattling down and the French *tricoleur* went up in its place. Ellen shouted something about wisdom in his ear, but he was concentrating on the steering, the set of the sail and the changeable wind.

The speed at which the two boats approached each other was tremendous. They were so close now that Dónal could see the crew of the French vessel standing ready at the main-deck guns, her officers watching him through telescopes. He took his right hand from the tiller and waved cheer-fully and he saw the officers nodding to each other.

The French bow-chasers were firing, water spouting on all sides of the *Iliad*. The motion of the waves and the speed of the ships made accuracy almost impossible, but once the enemy ship brought her broadside to bear, Dónal knew nothing would save them.

When the moment came that Dónal could see the faces of the French gunners, they were too close for the enemy guns to be brought to bear. Then they were almost under her bows. 'Helm's a-lee,' Dónal cried and swung the tiller. The *Iliad* passed through stays as smoothly as she had ever done and she paid off on to the other course. Then she was in the enemy ship's wind-shadow and all the canvas was flapping. 'Up topsail! Quick!' But Ellen and Alice had already begun to raise the sail and in a matter of moments it was in its place high up on the mast. It fluttered a moment, all eyes on it, then it filled and *Iliad* picked up speed again.

'Stand to your guns!' he shouted.

Even in the twilight Dónal could see the fury in the faces of the French officers. A flurry of activity broke out as gun crews changed sides and Dónal realised that his guess had been right – the French ship had enough men to fight one side only, a common enough occurrence in ships that had been a long time at sea. This was his chance.

'Right Ellen, Thomas, Alice. Stand to your guns. Steady. Wait for the word.' They took their places solemnly, watching Dónal for the signal. They were watched from on high by the astonished French. A huge noise filled the air, and smoke billowed from the ship. A ragged broadside from about one third of the French guns had passed high above their heads. 'Steady now.' Dónal waited till they were almost clear so that they could fire into the after-part of the ship. A lucky shot might strike the rudder or the steering chains and disable the French boat.

'Now, fire!'

They pulled the little lanyard that touched off the guns at the same moment and the cannon went off as regularly

as if they were trained man o'war's men. The tiny broadside struck the ship at close range but she went on her
way unchecked. The attack had been little more than a
nuisance. 'Stop your vents,' Dónal shouted, then realised
that his crew did not know what the vents were. No
matter. These guns did not get enough use to be damaged
by an unstopped vent.

The *Iliad* lurched violently as she came into the full force of
the wind and Thomas slipped downwards, coming to a stop
against the lee rail up to his knees in water. They had to
reduce sail.

'Down topsail.'

Then, 'Double reef, Ellen!' and they were struggling
with the mainsail. But now he saw the French officers
crowding the stern and one after the other they lifted
their hats to him.

'They're saluting us, lads!' A single gun went off and
a new hoist of signals went up. Dónal read them aloud.
'They're signalling *Happy return!*'

'How gallant!' cried Ellen. 'And what capital shooting!
Dear Dónal, it was capital! What a dashing attack!'

'A single gun to fire and all hands to remove their
hats.'

They set off one of the starboard guns and all hands
raised their hats and caps and cheered at the dwindling
stern of the enemy.

'I wonder now, do they see that,' said Alice pointing at a
heavy squall that was racing out of the west.

'The squall? Sure they have the men to reef her in two
minutes flat.'

'Not the squall, Dónal,' said Alice. 'The ship.'

Dónal saw it, a full-rigged ship racing before the wind, the black snouts of cannon run out on both sides, a British ensign flying from her truck. He thought he recognised her as the harbour guardship. Dónal could imagine the excitement aboard her – the eager talk of prize-money, the smell of the slow match between the decks, the light of the battle-lanterns, the calm voices of the officers. He saw the moment when the French captain realised the trouble he was in. He saw the furious urgency as the hands made sail and the ship swung round to run before the wind with all speed. Then the squall was upon themselves and they were fighting for their lives in blinding rain.

The mainsail came down completely and the jib too was hauled down onto the bowsprit. Then Dónal turned the *Iliad* and ran her off before the seas. Once he had the wind behind him the boat settled down and they had time to make the guns safe with double tackles, to tidy up the masses of sail that had been taken down, to clear the decks and bring the unused powder and shot below again. Time to consider their victory, for victory it had been – a tiny pleasure-yacht to run straight at a warship and even to fire on her and escape shot free! Had it ever been done before, Dónal wondered. Certainly not by the gentlemen of the Water Club!

9

BONAPARTE'S RETREAT

It took Dónal, Lieutenant Congreve and Achilles Daunt to
explain the situation to the Colonel. They pointed out that
Dónal had intended to return before sunset, that he could
not have expected the storm to become so violent, and
that even though he had a boat and could have sailed to
France in her, he had in fact returned. Still the Colonel
was annoyed and kept huffing on about boats being
unsporting and horses being much more reliable. In the
end, though, he was made to understand that Dónal had
not intended to break his parole, and all was forgiven. By
then, of course, Dónal had another worry. Captain Veasey
had got into trouble.

'It was when that other yacht came back . . . what was
her name? The *Columbine*. There was quite a crowd there,
all looking out to sea. They all knew, you know, that the
race was on, and they knew there was a bad storm and
that Daunt's grandchildren were in it. And then this
goddarned captain of the infantry came up to me and said
that you had run. A captain of the infantry!' Captain
Veasey said it as though to be in the infantry was in itself

an insult. 'Well, there wasn't a thing I could do, was there?' Captain Veasey looked sheepish.

Dónal shook his head forcefully. 'I can fight my own battles! I don't want you fighting over me.'

'But it was as much for America, boy. To think that upstart of a plodder, that mere ... infantry captain could insult an officer of the United States navy! Or even,' he added hastily, because neither he nor Dónal were quite officers of the navy, 'an American privateersman! I just flew into a rage. "I'll have you know sir," says I, "that officers of an honourable service do not run." "Well," says he, "Long has run from his parole anyway." 'You insult me and my country," I says. "Very well," says he. "What do you make of it?" I looked him right in the eye. "In that case," says I, "you will give me satisfaction." That confounded him, I declare.'

To "demand satisfaction" was the code for a duel. The captain of infantry had agreed readily and he and Veasey settled on a day and a time.

'Then I named you and the colonel for my seconds. That confounded him completely. "How can Long be your second," says he, "when he's half-way to America?" "Never fear, Captain," says I. "Dónal Long will be there on the appointed day at the appointed hour, and you will apologise with your dying breath."

'You named me as second?' Dónal said, furious at being drawn into the duel. Although the purpose of the seconds was simply to see that the fight was fair, nevertheless, like all right-thinking people, Dónal thought duels were pointless and wasteful. They were something that the older generation did. He did not believe any insult was serious enough to warrant the loss of a life. 'I want nothing to do with it!'

Now Captain Veasey looked like a hurt child. 'I did it for you, Dónal. The man was calling you a coward and a liar.'

Dónal knew it was Captain Veasey's affection for him that had made him suggest the duel. The Captain was a hot-tempered man who was completely loyal to his friends. Dónal knew he should appreciate this. He bit his tongue and spoke quietly a few moments later. 'I will be your second, Captain,' he said. 'Though God knows I would not have any harm come to you. I have grown fond of you locked up here. Awkward old curmudgeon that you are. And I have grown used to your snoring at night. I make no doubt I would not sleep without it now!' They both laughed.

'That's my lad,' Captain Veasey said. 'But you must call me Henry, now. I'm not a captain at present, and very shortly I may be in Davy Jones.' Davy Jones's locker was the sailor's name for the bottom of the sea. Dónal was tempted to say to the captain that if he was killed in a duel it was not a burial at sea that he would get, but a grave in the cemetery behind the fort. Instead he smiled and said he made no doubt but Captain Veasey was a better swordsman, having had plenty of play with cutlasses in the last few years over his seafaring career.

'Not swords, Dónal, pistols. I chose pistols.'

Dónal was shocked. 'You chose pistols against an infantry captain? Why, surely you must see the folly? The infantryman will be the better shot. You will be killed.'

The captain winked. 'I think not.' Even though Dónal

pressed him he would say no more on the point.

The duel was to be on the very next day at dawn, in a place called the Tansy Field, high up on the hill above the town. The colonel would convey Dónal and Captain Veasey to the spot in his own carriage. With such a high-ranking member of the military present there would be no question of the law becoming involved – although duelling had long since been illegal.

But before that there was the matter of the presentation. The Water Club, it appeared, had agreed to raise a subscription to honour Dónal and Ellen. They were invited to the Club rooms at West Beach for that afternoon.

Dónal worked hard to make his old uniform presentable, though his coat was threadbare and the seat of the trousers was shiny. His boots, that had looked so gallant and seamanlike in Baltimore last spring, were greyed by sea-salt and the left heel was coming loose. His cocked hat was so battered that he had to borrow Captain Veasey's. Nevertheless, at three o'clock Dónal made his way down to the town.

The people of the town went about their business, taking no notice of a poverty-stricken American prisoner. Dónal's heart was light. He was on his way to the Water Club, where he would be honoured for his part in saving the *Iliad*, and he was to meet Ellen Daunt.

He had been unable to get the girl out of his mind since they had returned. Even Captain Veasey's duel had not been worrying enough to banish her. He thought about her beauty, her courage, even her seamanship – although he found himself wondering at that. How many young men would praise a girl for her handling of a boat? It was not the usual thing in a young woman, but Dónal was a sailor and he respected that kind of thing. He valued and honoured Ellen Daunt for her mastery of the sailor's skills.

As he reached the door of the Water Club he was stopped by a hail from across the street. Turning, he saw Lieutenant Congreve, splendid in full dress uniform, making his way towards him.

'What? Are you bid to the Club as well, Congreve?'

'What ho, the hero,' Congreve said, slapping him on the back. 'How often will you distinguish yourself, may I ask? Will you ever give poor men like myself a chance to shine?'

Dónal laughed. 'You're mighty shiny now, anyway,' he said, pointing at the elegant uniform. 'You'll put me to shame!'

'And you should be ashamed,' joked Congreve. 'You stole away the fair Miss Daunt for two days and a night, when every officer in the harbour of Cork is willing to die merely for a glance from her eye.'

'Is she accounted fair then?' Dónal did not have experience in the matters of the heart. He only knew that he thought her the most beautiful person he had ever met, and a prime seaman into the bargain.

'Lord yes, old boy. You will see the gentlemen are like flies about her. She is the belle of the town.'

And there she was, as they came in through the doors, standing with her grandfather and four or five young naval and army officers. Dónal gasped when he saw her, for she was not wearing a smart evening gown such as any young lady might be expected to wear. She was wearing the blue uniform jacket of the Water Club, almost exactly like a navy uniform, over a gown of green lawn. Instead of a head piled high with hair, in the fashion of the time, she had coiled it into a long plait, almost exactly like a sailor's pigtail, and on her head was a very military-looking cocked hat.

'Why, here is our hero,' cried Achilles Daunt when he saw them enter. 'And Lieutenant Congreve! How do you, sirs? This is a great day!'

Before Dónal could say a word to Ellen they were drawn into the main room where the gentlemen of the Water Club were gathered. As they came through the door, the members broke into applause. There was much cheering and calls of 'What-ho, the hero!'

Dónal and Ellen were led to the top of the room and the Admiral, Lord Inchiquin, stepped forward. He began, in a loud voice, a long speech about the race, the terrible storm that had fallen on it, the seamanship required to save the boat, the courage of Ellen and Dónal, 'and indeed of young Thomas and Alice who alas have returned to school,' and a thousand other things. As his voice droned on, Dónal had a chance to look around at the friendly, smiling faces. How many of them would have bidden him the time of day ten years ago? Still, it would be unkind to think like that now. They were wealthy men, many of them landlords. They could no more imagine the life of someone like Dónal Long, the son of the poor fisherman, than he could imagine what their life of comfort and plenty was like.

This thought made him think of his love for Ellen Daunt. He realised at that moment that it was hopeless. Sailor or no sailor, Ellen Daunt was the granddaughter of an Irish shipowner. She would never marry him. She could not marry him. She could never even imagine marrying someone born in a cottage within sight of her father's house.

But now the Admiral was talking directly to him. What was he saying?

'... and so in token of our appreciation, nay of your wonderful heroic attack on the French ship of the line, and your care and safe keeping of the children of a dear friend of this Water Club, we would like to present you with this silver-hilted sword inscribed with the date, and with this club uniform to signify that you will always be an honoured member of the Water Club of the Harbour of Cork.'

Dónal found the sword and the uniform being pressed into his hands. Then he had to hand them to someone else because his hand was being shaken vigorously. Gentleman after gentleman shook it. He was dazed. Then they were talking about Ellen and she, in turn, was being presented with a silver platter.

Then, still dazed, he was handed a large cup of steaming punch and Ellen was standing beside him. Her eyes were shining and her cheeks were aflame. She held the silver platter clasped to her breast.

'How like you this, Mr Long?' And she laughed.

Dónal could not say how much he liked it. His head filled with ridiculously poetic phrases that he knew would sound utterly stupid. The only thing he could think of to say was, 'But are you permitted to wear the uniform of the club?'

'Oh yes.' She shook her finger at him. 'The Water Club has admitted women since the year seven. Only we are not permitted to wear the breeches.'

He wanted to tell her how beautiful she looked, how

her skirts of green lawn suited her, how she was the glory of his heart, but all he managed was, 'I . . . I am gratified to see you again, Miss Daunt.' He bowed like some foreign diplomat.

'Oh Dónal,' she said. 'There can be no Miss Daunt and Mr Long between us after the dangers we have passed through.'

'Then I may call you Ellen?' he asked. His heart was singing.

'You must never call me anything else, unless it is your dear friend.'

Congreve was there, raising his cup and pledging a toast 'To the fair Miss Daunt!'

'Miss Daunt has told me all about your adventures,' he said when he had emptied a glass of whiskey punch, and Dónal felt a sudden pang of jealousy. How did Congreve find the time and the opportunity to hear Ellen's story? But he was a gentleman like her grandfather. He would have been to her house. He probably visited regularly.

'Indeed,' Dónal said. 'And has she told you how she kept watch as well as any officer, how she managed the sails and fired the broadside at the French ship?'

'Oh, broadside,' Ellen smiled. 'It was but two popguns, Dónal. They would never even make an impression on the French and you know it.' They smiled together at the thought of it.

'It was hellish brave,' Congreve told them, 'to run at a ship of the line. I honour you all for it.'

Later Achilles Daunt took Dónal aside. 'You showed yourself to be brave and a good seaman, Mr Long.'

'It was no more than my duty. And my best estimate of where safety lay was in running under the guns of that ship. Had I known the guardship had come out of the harbour to chase her I would have behaved differently.'

'Nevertheless, it was cool. Cool, sir. A fine thing.'

They discussed the conduct of the *Iliad* in the gale. Dónal told him that she was as fine a ship as he had sailed in. Achilles Daunt was pleased by that. 'Now, sir, to more serious matters. My granddaughter, I may tell you, speaks glowingly of you.'

Dónal's heart skipped a beat. 'I was honoured to assist her.'

'It was more than that, lad. I have been to sea too, never forget that. My father put me to sea to learn my trade when I was a boy. I could not run a shipping line but that I know the ships myself.' He shook his head at the memory of it.

'Hearts open in the long watches of the night, Mr Long. I have known it. There is the sea and the wind, and the stars and moon to steer by. Two people alone on the deck of a ship must talk. They learn each other's past. A bond grows between them, the way two roses grown close together will entangle their branches.'

Dónal was uncomfortable now. No one had ever spoken like this to him before. Achilles Daunt was a blunt honest man but he was talking about love. Dónal was not used to it.

'What I mean to say is this: do not trifle. I am main fond of that granddaughter of mine. She is the apple of my eye. It is a grandfather's privilege to dote, and I dote on her. Do not trifle with her affections. If your heart is good, and you keep a place in it for her, speak up. But do not break hers. That's the end of it.'

Dónal searched for the right words.

'Mr Daunt, sir . . . I honour Miss Daunt. I treasure the long hours we were together. But I am a mere ship's officer. I am indeed, a prisoner. My childhood was not spent in the company of men such as these . . . ' he indicated the gentlemen of the Club. 'I am certain sir, that were I to speak I could not hold a place with even one of those officers that even now gather about her. I am afraid, sir, I can never speak. I must hold my peace, though it may break my heart.'

'Nonsense, sir,' exploded Achilles Daunt. 'Faint heart never won fair lady! Will you give up the field before you have even tried the enemy strength? I had thought better of you.'

'But sir,' said Dónal, 'do you really believe there is a chance for me?'

Achilles Daunt's eye twinkled and a smile curled the sides of his mouth. It was Ellen's smile, Dónal noticed, and she had the same colour of eye as her grandfather. 'You must seek the answer to that question elsewhere,' the older man replied.

Dónal was making his way back to the fort. He had left the gifts in the care of Lieutenant Congreve, not thinking them fitting for a prison guardhouse. It was a bright night and his heart was alive to the beauty of it, the silver shillings of moonlight on the rippling water, the ships' masts and spars silvered over, the sound of a lonesome voice singing in some foreign language across the bay, the calls of the anchor watches that all was well.

He went over and over Achilles Daunt's words, finding comfort in them at each examination. Certainly he would not have said them unless there really was some hope. Perhaps Ellen had confided in him. They were very close, almost like friends rather than grandfather and granddaughter. At any rate, he would try. He would not 'give up the field' as Achilles Daunt had said. On the first available occasion he would ask for her hand in marriage.

He had turned on to the steep lane that led up from the east beach when a man stepped from the shadows. Dónal could see immediately that it was the same man, the American spy, who had stopped him at almost the same point before. Would the man never leave him alone?

Then Dónal saw the glint of moonlight on the barrel of a pistol.

'Good night to you, Mr Long,' the spy said. 'I see you have been celebrating.'

'It is no business of yours,' Dónal replied, his head clearing rapidly.

'You are still set against helping your country?'

'If you mean spying, you are right. I am a sailor, not a spy. I detest your kind, sneaking around and doing the dirty work of other sneaks. Besides that, I have given my word of honour. Perhaps you do not have honour in your line of business?'

Even in the shadows Dónal could see that his words had struck home.

'Without my kind, you and yours would be useless.'

'That does not make your work any the more honourable.'

'Honour!' said the man bitterly. 'Enough of this. I have news for you. Napoleon Bonaparte surrendered five days ago. On the first day of March.'

With a shock Dónal realised that the surrender had taken place on the day of the race. That meant that the French ship was no longer at war, but because she was at sea she had not heard about the surrender.

'The news has only now reached Admiralty house here. You are one of the first to know it. Even your friend Congreve will not hear until tomorrow.'

'This makes no difference to me.'

'The British will now be able to turn their full attention to the war in America.'

Dónal had already worked that out for himself, his mind racing.

'We need information now more than ever. You must help us,' pressed the spy.

'I cannot, sir. I have given my word of honour. It is wrong even for you to ask me, and you know it.'

'All is fair in love and war, Mr Long. Would it surprise you to know that I am acquainted with a relative of yours?'

Dónal almost gasped. A relative? It could only be his uncle, a man so twisted and cowardly that he would do anything. He hated Dónal because he had taken the wrong side in the fight aboard the slave ship, and Dónal's side had won. Dónal thought he was still in Africa, where he had been put ashore. Then he remembered the evening he had first met Achilles Daunt, how he felt then that he was being followed, and the shape of the lame man scuttling into the tavern, how it had been at once familiar and strange. He knew now it must have been his uncle.

He made a valiant effort to show no emotion. 'Do you intend to hold me at pistol-point here for the night,' he enquired coldly.

'Ain't you going to enquire about your old uncle? He's told me all about your past. A word to the Admiralty office here and you would be on a ship bound for the penal colony of Australia, not back to America.'

'I think not,' Dónal said. He said it boldly but in his heart he was far from sure.

'I have no more time to talk to you now, Mr Long,' the spy said. 'I will meet you here tomorrow night just before sunset. I will bring your uncle, and you can talk it over. Bring me information and I won't go any further with what I know. Good night.'

He stepped aside, still holding the pistol, and Dónal walked past him. He had spoken calmly, but his mind was in turmoil. All his fears were about to be realised. Either he must spy for this man and betray his word of honour or he must risk losing his life, his liberty and Ellen Daunt. It was a frightening prospect.

10

DEATH IN THE GREY DAWN

The following day dawned cold and grey, a suitable morning for a duel, as Dónal remarked, stepping down from the Colonel's carriage. Dónal was first, followed by the colonel. Captain Veasey looked pale and grey and old in the morning light. Dónal had not noticed how frail his old captain had become in captivity. He had lost his sailor's sprightliness of step and his face was haggard.

The infantry captain had not yet arrived and Dónal took the chance to look about him. This Tansy Field was a steeply sloping meadow high up on the hill. From it he had a commanding view of the harbour – a majestic sight, crowded as he had never seen it before. He counted forty-one sail of ship within sight of where he stood and made no doubt that the quarantine anchorage and Whitegate Roadstead were all full too. This was as a consequence of the recent gales, which had kept in the merchantmen that were already there and had brought numerous fine ships scudding before the wind into the port, for the harbour of Cork was a refuge of the first class.

The sun was now just above the horizon, and a weak

light was spreading over the water and the hills. Dónal was just beginning to hope that the infantry captain might not, after all, appear, that perhaps his commanding officer had forbidden the duel, when he heard the sound of a carriage drawing up on the far side of a high ditch that bordered the northern side of the field. In a few moments the captain and his two seconds came in. With a shock, Dónal realised that one of the man's seconds was Lieutenant Congreve. Congreve waved cheerfully to him and immediately began to examine the ground.

'Come, my boy,' said the colonel. 'We must look to the weapons.'

Congreve introduced them to the others. There was Captain Turley of the infantry, the man who was to fight, and the other second was Lieutenant Davis of the marines. Davis had the box which contained the pistols and he flipped it open for them. The colonel picked both pistols out of the box, hefted them in each hand, examined the flintlock, cocked and pulled the trigger, examined the sights and looked down the barrel. 'A very handsome pair,' he said. 'Mr Davis, Mr Congreve, I believe we may begin.'

Davis carefully loaded each gun, under the eagle eye of the colonel, who was ensuring that the charges were the same, that the pistol-balls were true to shape and of equal weight. When the guns were loaded the seconds took one each and felt their weight again. It made Dónal shiver, knowing that one of the guns would cause the death of one of the men.

In the meantime, the two captains were pacing up and down at opposite ends of the field. Dónal went to speak to Captain Veasey.

'You could call the whole thing off now, before any blood

is shed over this ridiculous quarrel,' he said.

The Captain shook his head. 'I don't want bloodshed, Dónal. But that man called you a coward and a liar when he said you had run. He was proved wrong. He has not apologised.'

'You mean if he apologised you would not fight him?'

'Certainly I would not. I told you I don't want bloodshed.'

They talked for a while longer and then Dónal discussed it with the colonel, who was in complete agreement. 'It would be the honourable thing. Your captain is right.'

They marched over to the others and called Lieutenant Congreve and Lieutenant Davis.

'Captain Veasey's compliments. We are instructed to tell you that if Captain Turley would even now withdraw the unwarranted insult he gave and apologise in the presence of the seconds, Captain Veasey is prepared to withdraw his challenge and regard his honour as satisfied.'

'I will put your generous offer to Captain Turley,' Congreve said. But he returned a moment later to say that Captain Turley would not withdraw his remarks. 'And he expressly wished me to say that he would not apologise to a cowardly colonial rebel who was only trying to save his own skin.' Congreve was embarrassed. 'They were the precise words I was bidden to deliver, gentlemen. You may be assured that they are not my own sentiments.'

They brought this further insult to Captain Veasey, expecting his fierce temper to explode. Instead his face became even paler and he shook his head.

'The man is determined to take my life. What has driven him to it? I have done nothing to him. To say those things, here on the field of honour ... it is unthinkable. Well, may God have mercy on my soul.'

They walked to middle of the field. Captain Veasey and Captain Turley each chose a pistol. 'Now, gentlemen,' said the colonel, who had taken charge of things as the senior officer present. 'Stand back to back. Take twenty-five paces and then turn when I say "turn". From that time you may fire when you will. It is agreed, I take it, that the discharge of a single round will suffice?' The two captains nodded. 'Very well then. One shot each, no more.'

The seconds withdrew to a safe place, out of the field of fire.

'Now, gentlemen ... walk.'

The two captains walked away from each other. Dónal, his heart beating wildly, counted out twenty-five paces. Then both men stopped, still facing away, for what seemed like hours. The colonel called 'Turn'.

Everything seemed to happen at once.

Captain Veasey turned swiftly and discharged his pistol even before he had properly come round. Dónal knew that this was usually the sign of a nervous man; a shot fired like that could never hit its target. He was astonished to see the infantry captain fall backwards before he had even completed his turn. Captain Veasey's shot had struck home.

But now the infantry captain was propping himself up on his elbows. He had not yet fired his shot. Dónal saw him carefully sight along the barrel. Captain Veasey was honour-bound to stand still. If he ducked or ran now he would be called a coward for ever more.

Captain Veasey did not move.

Dónal saw the pistol levelled. He saw the face of Captain Turley, contorted with hatred and pain, the lips drawn back so that the teeth showed white. He saw the finger squeeze on the trigger, slow and deliberate. The pistol barked, a jet of fire and smoke shot from the barrel and the infantry captain fell back to the ground, exhausted by the effort of firing.

Captain Veasey made no sound but crumpled like a house of cards. Dónal and the colonel ran to him, while Congreve and Davis ran the other way.

'Henry! Henry, where are you hurt?' It was the first time Dónal had ever used his captain's first name. The captain was thrown down on his side, his right arm bent under him, his right leg drawn up. The pistol had fallen from his grasp and lay a few feet away, giving no sign of the injury that it had just done. Dónal felt despair – not for the first time – at the foolishness of men that drove them to war and to pointless duels over honour. Here was his friend Captain Veasey, dead of a pistol-ball from a boorish officer who should have had the decency to admit he was wrong.

But Captain Veasey was not dead. He sighed suddenly and rolled over on to his back. He looked up at Dónal and winked. 'Only a flesh wound, I think,' he said. Now that Dónal could see the other side of his head he noticed that the tip of his right ear was missing and blood was streaming down his neck.

'Are you shot?' he asked foolishly.

'Certain I'm shot,' snapped Captain Veasey. 'He shot my ear off, by the feel of it. But it's not mortal, man. The question is: is he shot? That's what I want to know.'

'That was a lucky shot!' Dónal cried. 'You knocked him down.'

'No luck, Dónal. I'm something of a marksman. I am used to the pistol. My father put me to it when I was a boy.'

At that moment Lieutenant Congreve came up, enquiring for Captain Veasey. When he learned that his wounds were slight he said, 'I congratulate you, sir. But if I could beg your seconds to assist me. I regret to say that Captain Turley has been seriously wounded.'

The ball had entered at a point just below his waist on his left-hand side. He was bleeding heavily and he was unconscious.

They all helped to carry the wounded man to the carriage and Davis drove it off at high speed towards the town, where a doctor might be found. The colonel went off in his carriage with Captain Veasey, to find the army surgeon who would look after the wounded ear, and Dónal and Lieutenant Congreve were left to find their own way down to Aeneas Lane's eating-house where they proposed to take their breakfast.

'I confess, this business seems so pointless to me. Two men shooting at each other like targets. I fail to see the honour in it.'

'Oh,' replied Congreve, 'it is dying out among our generation. At any rate, people like Turley deserve no better. I became his second only because no one else in the Cove of Cork would agree to do it. The man is abominable and deserved to be pistolled. Do not think twice about him. But stop, did you say that you were acquainted with Admiral Somerville? That is his flagship *Leander* just now threading through the anchorage.'

So it was. The old *Leander* was coming in on a topsail breeze, making her stately way towards Cove, the broad pennant of an admiral flying from her truck.

'The *Leander*,' Dónal said. 'I left many a good friend on her. I wonder if they are still living or have they found their way to Davey Jones's locker? I wonder if Gunner Best still rules the 'tween decks and if Thaddeus Gallahoo still sings the shanties?'

Lieutenant Congreve gave him a puzzled look and Dónal realised that the life of the 'tween decks was foreign to him. Lieutenant Congreve would not be likely to make friends with a mere gun-captain, or a shantyman.

'She has been in action against the French on the West Indies station. I should be surprised if she has not had heavy casualties. But perhaps your acquaintances may be still there.'

By the time they reached the quay, the *Leander* was already dropping her anchor off Admiralty House. Guns were going off to salute the return of Admiral Somerville and people were crowding down to the water's edge.

'We will hire a penny boatman and go out to her,' Dónal said. But Congreve excused himself and said he must pay his respects elsewhere. It was only later that Dónal realised that Congreve would have been embarrassed to see his friend greeted by common sailors. He slipped away into the crowd.

So Dónal called in a boatman and was rowed across to the *Leander*, which was by now settling into harbour routine. Her yards were teeming with men sent aloft to put 'a harbour stow' on the sails. Others were furiously washing and scrubbing the decks and polishing the brasswork. All her gunports were open to let the air in.

It was through an open gunport that Dónal found his way aboard. He climbed in and stood up to look around him. Immediately he was surrounded by curious and irritated sailors.

'Wot you want, mate?'

'Oo the 'ell are you?'

'Strike me blind if it ain't a Yankee! Wot you gonna do? Take the ship?'

Dónal smiled and held up his hands to show that he was unarmed.

'I'm looking for an old friend of mine,' he said. 'Gunner Best his name was ...'

'Who's asking for me?' A big voice from somewhere in the gloom of the gun deck.

'Is it Gunner Best?' said Dónal. A big man pushed his way through the staring crowd to stand before him, hands on hips. Dónal knew him immediately. He was the same burly, gruff man that he had known as a boy. The same open face.

'Don't you know me, Besty?' he said. When Gunner Best shook his head in puzzlement, Dónal said, 'Dónal Long, remember? You and Charlie Madden rescued me from a sinking fishing smack.'

Suddenly Gunner Best's face cracked into a smile. 'Dónal, boy!' he roared. He clasped Dónal's hand and shook it till Dónal thought it would come off. 'Look at you,' he said. 'Is that an officer's uniform? Yankee too, by God! Lads,' he said turning to the crew, 'this is the lad I often told you about. This is my old shipmate Dónal Long.'

Then everyone was shaking his hand and telling him they all knew his story. A thin wizened man advanced and tipped his forelock and said, 'Ship's carpenter John Fly, beggin' your pardon, sir.'

'John Fly?' said Dónal. 'John Fly, of course I remember you. You made me my sea-chest and I still have it at home in Baltimore.' Tears came suddenly to John Fly's eyes and he had to wipe them away.

'For shame, John Fly, ship's carpenter! Blubberin' again!' said Gunner Best.

Just then they heard a strong voice strike up an old favourite, 'I'm homeward bound and I'll draw me pay.'

Dónal stopped to listen. 'Is it Thaddeus Gallahoo?'

'It is begod!' said the shantyman, stepping through the crowd to shake Dónal's hand and changing his tune to 'Captain Somerville and the Frenchman,' a song about the sea-battle Dónal had fought in on this very ship the *Leander*.

11

GUILTY

In the week that followed Dónal renewed all his old acquaintances. He and Besty walked together for hours on end, talking about old times and old friends and strolling along the docks or out into the country. They ate, together with John Fly and Thaddeus Gallahoo, in Lane's eating-house. Ellen Daunt met them too and shook hands with them all, making Thaddeus Gallahoo shy and bringing tears to John Fly, who declared her 'the most loveliest creature he had seen since he saw the queen of Tahiti', which Ellen took as a great compliment. They were all convinced that Dónal and Ellen were engaged to be married and whenever her name was mentioned Thaddeus and John Fly would wink and elbow each other and say that they 'knew what way the wind lay' and could 'tell a smart brig by the cut of her jib' and various other seamanlike ways of telling him that they knew more than they said.

Once John Fly had made a little speech to Ellen, saying that as they had been shipmates with Dónal they wished to tell her that he was a decent man, though now an American, and that he would do honour to any marriage, and that she could not find a better man this side of the world, unless it be John Fly himself, who, though old, was still the best damn ship's carpenter in the Navy. John Fly had taken a drop too much and the speech wandered off into comparisons between his workmanship and that of other 'lubberly plank-nailers and time-servers that he might mention' who could not 'fish a mast if their life depended on it'. But Ellen only laughed and said that she was sure Dónal was the very picture of decency and that John Fly was a most able carpenter, and in that way the whole thing was forgotten. Still Dónal was in dread of what they would say to Ellen, expecting at any moment that one of them would come straight out and ask her when the wedding would be, which they would think the best of sport, but which he was sure would shock Ellen.

But she did not seem to notice any of their sallies. She would take Dónal's arm and stroll beside him, listening to their talk and marvelling at their stories, which Dónal noticed, were full of bigger and bigger battles and more dangerous storms the more they talked.

'Oh, they are full of tall tales,' he said to her one evening. 'Which we might call lies except that they are merely for fun. A more honest man you could not find than Gunner Best, nor a truer friend. And as for the others, there is not a wicked bone in their bodies.'

'They esteem you highly,' she said, looking into his eyes. 'They think you the best of friends.'

'As I am, I hope,' he said. 'For they saved my life once. I hope I may never forget that.'

'Are you happy, Dónal?' she asked. 'Sometimes you seem cast down. I know not what may be the cause of it.'

'Oh, Ellen,' he said. 'These are the happiest days of my life but for my captivity. If I were a free man I could count myself the luckiest on earth.'

It was towards the end of the second week that Dónal was introduced again to Captain Somerville, now Admiral, and that good man expressed his delight that Dónal had fulfilled all his hopes.

'I knew from the first time I saw you that you would rise in the world,' the Admiral said. 'My only regret is that like many another caught up in the terrible events of that year of '98, you have not been able to serve your true king. Had the country been governed with more care and less cruelty you might even now be an officer on this ship.'

Dónal shook his head. 'I am an American now, sir. I have no king. And though we have fought on opposite sides I can never consider you an enemy. I honour you for your kindness to me and I will never forget the friendship I found in this ship.'

'Yes, yes,' said the Admiral, well pleased with that speech. 'But pray, finish the tale you began earlier. Begin at where you first saw the storm coming on you. I have seen such squalls in my time on the West Indies Station. A most prodigious dangerous squall.'

Dónal was sitting in the Admiral's great cabin, a room that stretched right across the stern of the *Leander*. One wall, the part that looked out behind the ship, was made entirely of glass. It was through that same glass that he had seen the last of his father's boat, the *Ellen Brice*, before she sank all those years ago. Now he saw a boat pulling towards them, across the water from Cove. A man in ordinary clothes sat in the stern sheets, his beaver hat pulled low over his eyes, a cloak held tight around his shoulders, a strange sight on a bright warm day.

As Dónal finished his story he heard this boat bump gently against the side of the *Leander* and heard someone come aboard. Before long there was a knock at the Admiral's cabin and an officer came in.

'Gentleman to see you, sir,' he said, and the gentleman thrust past him into the cabin at the same moment.

He swept his hat off and threw his cloak back from his face. 'Tobias Wilson,' he said. 'At your service, Admiral.'

The name did not at first mean anything to Dónal but he saw, with shock, the vicious gleam in the eye, the snarl on the lips, the haughty tilt of the head, and recognised the face of his hated enemy, Lieutenant Tobias Wilson, late of the *Leander*. Lieutenant Wilson had sworn to destroy him many years ago. He had planned the murder of Dónal's friend Charlie Madden. He had been first officer here, but Admiral Somerville had disliked him and had put him off the ship, saying there was no place in the navy for such a cruel officer.

'Good God!' Admiral Somerville cried. 'Wilson! How dare you come into my cabin. I'll have you thrown overboard, by God! I'll have you flogged.'

'I think not, Admiral Somerville.' He said the word *Admiral* in such a way as to suggest that he had very little respect for the rank. 'I believe I am in my rights. You have before you a prisoner of war on parole. That is a military matter, of course. But Dónal Long is also a felon and a criminal. Charges have been laid against him, to wit, attempting to procure the escape of notorious rebels, membership of the proclaimed United Irishmen, escape from prison, communicating with an American spy. Here are the warrants and papers.' He produced a sheaf of papers from his inside pocket. 'You will find they are perfectly in order.'

'Don't talk rubbish in my cabin, sir. I cannot abide it,' Admiral Somerville snapped.

'You will find the warrants in order.'

'Who, pray, are you, to come into my cabin demanding people out of my ship?'

'You might say I work for the Secretary of State. My official capacity need not concern you. I have demanded the prisoner. You will produce him or I shall seek redress ashore.'

The Admiral was examining the warrants but even from where he sat Dónal could see that they were official. There would be no denying them. The moment he had feared ever since his capture had finally come and Wilson, of all men, was the one to bring it about. No matter how hard he tried he would not find it easy to escape this time.

The Admiral looked up suddenly, a spark of under-standing in his eye. 'A spy, by God,' he said. 'That's what you are, isn't it Wilson? A sneaking spy and informer. A coward and a sneak. Well, you have found your place in life at last. No merchant captain you, no hard work or honest living. You will make your way over the ruined lives and families of decent people. I would respect the lowliest man on this ship more than you, even the deserter who at least has the courage to run away. But you – you profit by the weakness of your fellow man. You are beneath contempt.'

Tobias Wilson sniggered. 'Decent people, Admiral? I hardly think the people I meet are decent. Traitors, preachers of sedition, plotters against the lawful government of His Majesty. Not a decent man among them. They generally finish at the end of a rope.'

'You are little better than a common thief-taker!'

'As for their families, they are none of my care. They may go upon the parish or starve, and they deserve it for harbouring the criminal. Which, if I may say so, is what you are doing at present. A very dangerous practice, harbouring a criminal.'

'Is that a threat, sir?'

'Not at all, Admiral. But I must press you to hand over the prisoner Dónal Long. His arrival at Cork Gaol is eagerly awaited.'

Nothing is a secret on a ship, with thin walls of oak and five hundred men to listen. When Dónal came on deck, accompanied by Wilson and Admiral Somerville, Gunner Best and the others blocked the way. There was anger in every face, and a steely determination.

Tobias Wilson was surprised and clearly shocked. He stopped as he came through the companionway and took a step backwards, looking furtively around for a means of escape. But Admiral Somerville stepped forward and spoke quietly to the men. He told them that Dónal was lawfully taken, that he must stand trial at Cork Assizes, that Wilson had all the proper warrants and papers. He commended them for their loyalty to Dónal.

'But you must not raise friendship above the law of the kingdom. The law is all that stands between us and destruction. Would you have another Spithead Mutiny? Would you have me hauled before an Admiralty Court and made to account for the behaviour of my men, men whom I trusted and who fought with me side by side in many a brave action. For shame,' he told them, 'you are not mutineers but loyal men. Stand aside there, we must walk through.' And they stood aside and made a passage, a narrow one, that permitted Dónal to walk to the steps that led to the boat and Wilson to walk after him. A deathly silence had fallen over the ship so that they could hear the creaking of the anchor ropes in the hawse-holes and the straining of the rigging.

As Dónal passed Gunner Best he saw tears in his old friend's eyes. 'Cheer up, Besty,' he whispered. 'I have been in prison before this.'

They passed on in silence and went down the steps and into the waiting boat. When Wilson gave the order to shove off, Dónal looked up and waved. He saw Best staring down on him, his face a mask of sadness. Beside him stood Thaddeus Gallahoo and John Fly. As the boat pulled away, Thaddeus began to sing:

> Oh I thought I heard the old man say,
> Leave her Johnny, leave her . . .

It was a slow old hauling shanty and the crew quickly joined in. As Dónal's boat pulled slowly between the anchored ships, the voices of his friends followed him and he did not lose them until he was walking up the steps of Columbine Quay.

In all that time Tobias Wilson had not said a word, only stared at him, his face white with spite and triumph. But when they were at last on dry land again he began to speak.

'You thought you had made a fool of me, Long,' he said. 'But a peasant like you does not have the brains for it. I shall see you hang now. I shall stand at the foot of the gallows and laugh in your face.' He looked at Dónal's coat and sneered. 'An American officer! You are little better than a pirate.'

'I ask only that I be allowed to send word to my captain who is at Carrignafoy Fort.'

'Most certainly not,' said Wilson. 'These gentlemen would be disappointed if you did not come with them.' He indicated two men who were watching them from the door of a coach. 'See, they have a coach ready for you. A grand officer like you must have a coach.'

'You take great pleasure in this, Mr Wilson. It was ever so. You were a cruel officer and now you are a cruel spy. But your cruelty surely cannot extend to my friends? They are innocent of any wrongdoing in your regard. Pray, let me write two notes to leave with Aeneas Lane in his eating-house. The good man will see they go to the right places.'

Wilson simply waved to the two men and they sprang down from the coach and rushed towards him. In a moment they had pinioned his arms behind his back. Then Tobias Wilson went to the coach. He took out some chains. He held them up and Dónal saw that they were a pair of convict's leg-irons.

Dónal Long, late first officer of the *Shenendoah*, was brought to Cork Gaol in irons and thrown into that black hole from which the light of day was permanently excluded, and where his friends could only with great difficulty find him out. He was tried at the next Assizes. The charges were as Tobias Wilson had said: attempting to procure the escape of notorious rebels, membership of the proclaimed United Irishmen, escape from prison, with the addition of the taking of an illegal oath. The charge of communicating with an American spy was dropped for lack of evidence. But any one charge was sufficient to bring a death sentence.

Tobias Wilson gave his evidence: that he had received information that Dónal Long had communicated with fleeing rebels in 1798 in the city of Waterford, that his father had been a member of the United Irishmen, that he had been taken into custody by Captain Turner of the West Waterford Yeomanry, that he had escaped from the prison van with the assistance of several other rebels, that he had somehow procured the release or escape of his uncle and that he himself had escaped eventually to take up arms against His Majesty in the service of the Americans.

This evidence could not persuade the jury to find him guilty. They disliked Tobias Wilson and hung their heads and shuffled their feet and glanced at Dónal from time to time. Tobias Wilson seemed to have failed.

But another witness was called. He was Michael Long, Dónal's uncle. He swore to tell the truth and then told more lies than Dónal had ever before heard from any man. He said that Dónal was indeed a sworn rebel, that he had secret dealings with the rebels, that all that Wilson said was true. Furthermore he swore that Dónal had tried to get him to take information about Carrignafoy Fort to American spies.

Dónal watched his uncle from the dock where he stood. The man was old and bent, his face twisted by wounds and spite. He trembled as he spoke and wept copiously as he told the court how hard Dónal had been to him in Africa.

'You are a pitiful dog,' Dónal thought, 'not fit for the company of human beings, a coward, an informer and a liar. You have betrayed your own family.'

But such thoughts would not pass as evidence. When he stood in the witness box himself, all he could do was deny what was false. That he had escaped from prison he did not deny, yet he would not name those who had helped him, for they were the very friends he had lately met in the *Leander*. He could not name the people who came in the dark of night to break the door in the prison-van, because their leader was Gunner Best and Admiral Somerville had been a party to it as well.

Achilles Daunt came forward and gave it as his opinion that whatever his past, Dónal Long was a decent man now and would never have broken his parole by sending information to the Americans. Mr Uniacke Fitzgerald and Lieutenant Congreve said the same. They asked the jury to weigh their testimony against that of Mr Wilson, a government spy, and Michael Long, a low coward who would betray his own nephew.

The jury did weigh up the evidence and their verdict was guilty on all charges. Then the magistrate put on his black cap and looked solemnly at Dónal. The crowd in the courtroom gasped and the sailors shouted their anger. But the judge spoke evenly.

'Dónal Long, you have been found guilty by a jury of your peers of the most heinous and terrible crimes. The sentence of this court is that you should be taken to the place from whence you came, and within three weeks, taken thence to a place of public execution where you shall be hanged by the neck until dead. May God have mercy on your soul.'

12

THE REPRIEVE COMMITTEE

The small group of people that styled itself the 'Dónal Long Reprieve Committee' was holding its customary weekly meeting. The venue was the home of Mr Achilles Daunt. Present were: Achilles Daunt himself; the beautiful Miss Ellen Daunt who was the youngest in years but had proved to be strongest in spirit of all of them; Admiral Henry Coyle Somerville; Lieutenant Congreve, now a staff officer at Admiralty House; and finally the honourable Murrough O'Bryen, second son of Lord Inchiquin, representing his father, who had taken an interest in the case but was unable to attend regularly at meetings.

As for Dónal Long himself, he languished in Cork Gaol, a sentence of death awaiting him if the long drawn out appeal process did not work. His spirits were good, the committee was told at the outset of the meeting, his courage held: his health had recovered, fortunately, for the bout of influenza that was now sweeping the gaol had killed seven prisoners. This news came from Miss Daunt, who had been his most frequent visitor.

'He has made friends there,' she told them. 'For Dónal

is well able to make friends. There is a little wasted boy to whom he is teaching his letters and who keeps his mind occupied. And there is another man, a forger I think, who has read much and they often talk together.'

The others shook their heads in wonder that a ship's officer should be reduced to a ragged boy and a forger for company.

'But I fear, gentlemen,' she said, 'that unless we can give him some hope he will sink into despair, and then God alone knows how he will fare.'

'The summer comes on,' Achilles Daunt said gloomily. 'Last summer's typhus went hard with prisoners. They died like flies, the poor devils.'

'Yet,' said Lieutenant Congreve, optimistic as always, 'all is not lost. We have stout allies. Keep up your hearts, my friends. Dónal will be restored to us, you will see.'

Admiral Somerville coughed and said that he earnestly hoped it was true. 'Let us review the situation,' he said, very much as he would say to a meeting of fleet captains before a sea battle. 'Let each one of us make a report and when we are in possession of the facts we will discuss how to proceed.' Admiral Somerville had gradually taken on the role of chairman of the 'committee' and he approached the task with the mind of one practised in campaigning and strategy.

The first to report was Murrough O'Bryen. 'I have in my possession at long last the reply of the Chief Secretary. I regret to say that my letter does not seem to have changed his mind. He writes to me that he never interferes in a judgement of the court. Not in any circumstances.'

'Damn liar!' cried Admiral Somerville.

'But sure,' said Murrough O'Bryen, 'we all know that if the jury had found him not guilty the Chief Secretary would have interfered in great haste.'

They all nodded their heads. They had seen it in the past. Everyone knew stories of juries bought and paid for by the crown, who convicted innocent men and women because they were told to, and judges who were so afraid of losing their pensions that they directed juries to bring in whatever judgement the Chief Secretary wanted.

'However,' Murrough O'Bryen added, 'there is a jot of hope that we may take encouragement from. I wrote to him, you know, that to our certain knowledge Michael Long had perjured himself on at least one point. The Chief Secretary says in his letter that he does not believe us. However he adds that if we can undermine the evidence of Michael Long he will look at the case again.'

'In that event,' Admiral Somerville said, 'it makes the work of Lieutenant Congreve all the more important.'

Lieutenant Congreve glanced at the page of notes on his lap. 'I have, as you know, an able assistant in Gunner Best of the *Leander*. He is a stout friend of Dónal. He has organised those seamen that Admiral Somerville has released from duty in a most extraordinary fashion. I declare they are a veritable secret service in themselves. They go up and down the country seeking news of the old rogue. They have been into every town and village in the County Cork, I daresay. However, to date I regret to report they have found no trace of him. Michael Long has gone to earth, we know not where.'

This report was greeted by sad faces. Ellen seemed almost in tears.

'Mr Daunt, how say you?' Admiral Somerville asked.

Old Achilles Daunt cleared his throat and smiled weakly at Ellen.

'I have discovered this confounded yeoman, Captain Turner.'

Ellen said, 'The one who arrested Dónal in '98?' Her voice betrayed her excitement. Even to find the man was something. Even if he proved as vile and wicked as everyone said he was.

'The very one,' Achilles Daunt said.

'By all accounts he was a disgrace to the name of Englishman,' Admiral Somerville said. 'A torturer and a murderer. His kind will not help us. Why, I'm sure he would rather see Dónal hanged than released.'

'There I have the advantage of you,' Achilles Daunt said, his eyes beginning to twinkle. 'For you see, I have made a discovery.'

Now they were all listening intently. Lieutenant Congreve leant forward, Ellen held her breath.

'Out with it, sir,' Admiral Somerville cried impatiently. 'Let us hear your discovery by all means.'

Achilles Daunt cleared his throat again. 'Captain Turner of the West Waterford Yeomanry is no more.'

They all groaned.

'Confound the man for dying!' cried Admiral Somerville, slapping his hand upon the arm of his chair.

Achilles Daunt laughed. 'By which I mean that he is Captain Turner no more, sir,' he said. 'He is plain Turner now. Very plain indeed. The man has become a monk.'

This last remark was greeted with an astonished silence. Lieutenant Congreve was the first to break it. 'A monk, sir? It is scarcely to be believed!'

'The murdering torturer?' cried Admiral Somerville. 'Do not talk rubbish on my quarterdeck sir,' he cried, forgetting that he was in Achilles Daunt's drawing room and not on a quarterdeck at all.

'It is astonishing, I know,' Achilles Daunt said. 'But it is true. Captain Turner is now Brother Turner. He is a monk of the Franciscan Order, a very poor and humble man indeed. Very sorry for his past cruelties. He goes about in a plain brown habit with only sandals on his feet.'

'I have never heard of such a thing,' said Admiral Somerville.

'But, sure, he will never come into court and swear that he wronged Dónal. And if he did, he would scarce be believed,' said young Murrough O'Bryen, who had never heard of such a thing himself.

'But still,' cried Ellen, 'it is the very best of news. It is something to hope for. Now for the first time I begin to believe we may succeed.'

'But, sure, he will not remember a small boy out of all the boys and men he imprisoned in that terrible year,' said Murrough O'Bryen.

'On the contrary, my friend,' Achilles Daunt said. 'He remembers every single one. He gave me to know certain details of Dónal's arrest that were exact. He will make a most reliable witness.

'But still,' said Murrough O'Bryen, 'there must be others to come in and swell the evidence. We must try to find the others.'

Just then there was a knock at the door and Mary the

maid walked in. She curtsied to the company and said, 'Beggin' your pardon Mr Daunt, but the English sailorman is after coming. Will I bring him up?' She giggled and curtsied again to cover it up. Ellen Daunt had found her in a cell in Cork Gaol on one of her visits. She was sixteen years old and already a widow. Her husband had died the year before in an accidental explosion at the gunpowder factory. To feed her baby daughter she had stolen a piece of bacon and the court had sentenced her to two years for this crime. When Ellen found her she had just been told that her baby daughter had died of influenza at the orphanage. It was her wailing that brought Ellen to her cell.

'Do. Send him up, Mary,' Ellen said. And turning to the company she said, 'And let us pray that he brings good news.'

The heavy tread of Gunner Best was heard on the hall and presently he stepped in. He made an imposing figure in that elegant drawing room. He was tall, well over six feet, with brown hair bleached almost white by the sun. He kept it tied back in a long pigtail, as was the fashion among sailors. He wore a blue jacket and white duck trousers. At his waist was a broad leather belt into which was stuck a wicked-looking knife. Ellen stood up to welcome him and he took her hand gently and smiled at her. Then he tipped his forelock to the Admiral and told them that he had just come from the harbour.

'What news, Best?' the admiral asked.

'Good news, in faith,' said Best. 'We have found the rascal.'

Ellen gasped and had to sit down quickly. She looked

up from the chair with an eager face as Best explained to them that Michael Long had simply gone home to his own place, the very thing they thought he would never do. They were so long in finding him because he had gone on foot and had spent most of his time drinking in taverns. By now he had spent all of the money with which Wilson had bribed him to give evidence.

'There is something else,' he said. 'He has fallen out with Wilson. He says Wilson promised him fifty guineas if he gave evidence against Dónal. But he says that when the trial was over he gave him only ten.'

Murrough O'Bryen clapped his hands together and said, 'I declare we will win for sure now!'

The admiral was a little more cautious. 'The man has perjured himself once. What court will believe that he is not perjuring himself again?'

'Ah, but you see, you miss the best of it,' Gunner Best told them. 'I laid him aboard in a cheap tavern near Aghada. He was well drunken and he talked too much and too loud. There was a gentleman drinking in the next room, wetting his whistle after a long journey you understand. His name was Nicholas Furney. He heard everything and since he knew Dónal's father many years ago, he will swear to every word of it. He will give his affidavit tomorrow if Mr Daunt will send a clerk and a notary. So he says.'

Murrough O'Bryen said that he knew Nicholas Furney and knew him to be an honest man.

Achilles Daunt said that he would send the notary by the green boat to Ballymonas in the morning. Lieutenant Congreve was so excited that he stood up and clapped

Gunner Best in the back and said that he was an 'excellent fellow'.

'This is the very best of news,' he said. 'What, Ellen? The very best?'

But Ellen did not answer. She had turned away and was gazing steadily out of the window. A soft rain had swept in over the harbour, obscuring the ships in the anchorage. But it was not the mist that prevented her from seeing the ships. It was her own tears.

13

A Full Moon Rising

Dónal Long emerged from his prison cell to the cold light of a wintry April afternoon. It was a day to make people think of warm clothes and hot fires. But Dónal's clothes were thin and threadbare and he had not seen a warm fire in quite a long time. His face was thin and grey and there were dark rings around his eyes. He had suffered from, and recovered from, a severe bout of influenza, and still had a bad cough. He had fared better than many of his fellow prisoners who now filled pauper's graves. He had seen the work of the Irish court system at its worst – the man sentenced to death for smuggling, only to be reprieved and transported for fourteen years to Australia instead; the young woman sentenced to two years' hard labour for the theft of a handkerchief; the mother and child dying of consumption, sentenced to six months for stealing meat; the man serving six months for sedition, merely for writing a letter attacking the government. There were also hardened criminals who deserved something of what they got, murderers, thieves and such, but Dónal had often found them as humane as their gaolers, sometimes a great deal more humane.

He emerged from the gates of Cork Gaol with a small bundle under his arm and a young boy by his side. He was met by a small party of his friends – the reprieve committee lacking only Admiral Somerville, who was away on naval business. Everyone shook his hand and congratulated him on his release. They would all have liked to travel down in Dónal's carriage but it was not permitted. Achilles Daunt, with much winking and nudging and broad looks, shooed them all, including Dónal's little friend from prison, into the fine carriage of Murrough O'Bryen. Thus it was that Dónal and Ellen Daunt were left alone to come down in her father's carriage. As they made their slow way down over the hills of Cork down into 'the flat of the city' as Cork people say, Ellen and Dónal clasped each other's hands and talked earnestly of the past, and the future.

From Ellen Dónal learned for the first time that his appeal had been entirely successful and that the court had ruled that the evidence of his uncle was unreliable. As a consequence, since Wilson's charges had been based on the word of Dónal's uncle, Wilson's case was thrown out too. Brother Turner's evidence had finally made up the judge's mind. He set Dónal Long free. For once, justice had triumphed.

The war with America was over. Dónal was no longer a prisoner but neither had he any employment or money. Captain Veasey had gone back to America with the first exchange of prisoners and Dónal had received a letter from him to say that a good deal of their prize-money had been lost when the bank they invested it in had collapsed. He had not heard from Captain Veasey since then and so he had no idea if anything had been saved. He had made up his mind that he would act as though there were no money left. In that way, if it happened that he was not a beggar after all, it would come as a pleasant surprise.

'Now you see me,' Dónal said to Ellen Daunt, 'a penniless man. I have no ship to my name, no money, no land, no prospect of the future. All I can say is that I love you more than life itself and if you will wait for me, I will go to sea again and with luck I will get a command in time. But I know I do not have the right to ask you this. Except for the words that have passed between us these last months I would never dare to say it. I know Lieutenant Congreve loves you too, and he is a far better man than me.'

Tears came into Ellen's eyes, but they were tears of anger. 'You foolish man!' she cried, so loudly that the conversation stopped short in Murrough O'Bryen's carriage, twenty yards ahead of them. 'Is it Lieutenant Congreve you think I love? Is it for his sake I have laboured all this time to have you freed? How did you ever navigate a ship when you cannot navigate a simple conversation!'

In Murrough O'Bryen's carriage Lieutenant Congreve heard his own name and his face turned purple. To cover his embarrassment he blew his nose loudly and declared that it was 'monstrous cold for the time of year' in the tone of voice that he reserved for shouting at distant sailors who were not doing their duty.

By the time the carriage had left the hills, Dónal knew that Ellen Daunt would always love him, that she had never any intention of loving anyone else, that she had loved him since the night of the storm.

So did everyone in Murrough O'Bryen's carriage and a good many passers-by. Ellen Daunt was not in the mood for ladylike quietness. Dónal thought her the most forthright young lady he had ever met, and considering that he had not met above three or four young ladies, he might be forgiven for thinking so.

'But what is the name of that young ragamuffin who came out with you, Dónal?' Ellen asked. 'He is a mere scarecrow, the poor child.'

'His name is Denis Hegarty,' Dónal said. 'He got seven years for stealing a ham and a pound of mutton. He was so cheerful in prison that we all looked after him. He was wont to sing songs for us and tell us tales, so that he often cheered us in the worst of times. '

'Is he the boy you were teaching?'

'The very same. I am teaching him his ABCs. Listen, love, this is what he said to me. I commenced teaching him his letters in the time-honoured fashion of the sea. I taught him the song that goes, "A is the anchor that hangs by the bow, B is the bowsprit that bends like a bow." He interrupted me and, says he, "I know right well what an anchor is, but what is an A". I knew then that he was woefully ignorant. I have made up my mind to educate him to the sea. When I get an appointment on a ship he will be my cabin boy, and if not that, I will train him to the trade.'

'How came he to be out the same day as you?'

'Oh, his ticket was up this week past but he made up his mind not to leave until I did, so they could not shift him. The governor himself begged him to go, but every time they tried to catch him he scampered off and made such a noise that all the prisoners shouted for him to be left alone. The governor was afraid there would be a riot if he did not leave him.'

'And what of the other man, the forger?'

Dónal's face paled suddenly and he looked out the window at the passing streets. 'Oh, he passed away on Monday last. It was the influenza took him.'

Just then the carriage halted outside the Oyster Tavern. They all got down and hurried inside, followed by a very puzzled Denis Hegarty. The rain had begun to come down in icy sheets and it poured from the rooftops into the narrow lane that led to the tavern. They were all glad to stand close to the fire in the little private room that Achilles Daunt had reserved for their celebration. In a moment a servant in a green jacket, with a sour expression on his face, had put a glass of wine in every hand. The servant looked with distaste at Denis Hegarty and would have pushed him out the door but that he was stopped and told to fetch a glass of milk.

Dónal called out to the boy to step in. 'Gentlemen, Ellen, this is Denis Hegarty, who is a good lad and was a great help to me in prison. He has sworn to follow me in whatever ship I sail. He will be my apprentice.'

'That I will, Master Long,' he said, and everyone smiled and clapped him on the back and said he would do well so, for Dónal Long was a good sailor.

'Were you ever at sea, young man?' Achilles Daunt enquired.

'Only so far as to cross the river,' said Denis Hegarty, 'and that by the Parliament Bridge.'

They all roared with laughter at the joke. Then Achilles Daunt waved them to silence.

'My friends, I believe I speak for everyone when I declare that we are all heartily glad to have Dónal Long back among us. I know I speak for one in particular when I wish him good health and a happy future. Now, it is not for nothing that I have given my small talents to this committee. Not for nothing. I have an interest in Mr Long you see. Long ago, when he was still a prisoner of war, I set my eye on him. At that time, all I knew of him was that he was the mate of a fine Yankee schooner. I spoke him on the subject, yes, and he gave me a good account of himself. But more than that, for I am a trading merchant as you know, he gave a good account of these same schooners, how fast they are, and weatherly and so forth.'

They were all silent now, but there was the shadow of a smile on every face. Dónal looked around him and his heart was full to have such friends.

'To make a long story short, I was determined from that time to make him captain of the first schooner I could buy.' There was a gasp of surprise. 'And I may tell you now, that ever since the day the late war ended I have had one in build on the Chesapeake Bay. Supervised by our old friend Captain Veasey, now a retired gentleman of that place.'

Ellen clapped her hands together and jumped up and down with glee. 'Oh grandfather!' she cried.

'Yes, a fine schooner. She will be fitted out and ready to sail by the first day of summer, so I am told.' He turned directly to Dónal and held out his hand. 'Dónal, will you be master of her? She will be the first fast schooner to trade out of Cork. I have her down for the West Indies run.'

Dónal was overcome. So much joy at once. All he could do was nod his head three or four times and shake Achilles Daunt's hand, all the while staring at Ellen.

'I take it you mean to say yes,' Achilles Daunt said, his

face creased in a broad smile. 'Then, in that case may I be the first to call you Captain Long?'

Now they were all shaking his hand. He smiled at them and thanked them in a daze. When they were finished he looked hard into Ellen's eyes and she looked back at him. He was asking her the one question that he wanted answered. She took his arm and led him to the table, and as they walked she whispered, 'Yes Dónal. I will indeed,' though he had not uttered a word aloud.

It was three hours before they could escape together, Dónal and Ellen. Until then they ate and drank with the rest of them, but their thoughts were elsewhere. They heard speeches from almost everyone, and when Admiral Somerville came in, having hurried by postchaise from Cove, they had to listen to his words of congratulations too. The old admiral's voice boomed in their ears as he treated the friends to the kind of stirring address he usually gave to a group of captains who had just won a particularly dangerous battle.

'Never knew an action like it!' he declared 'Caught them off guard, what! By God, there's no spy or lackey or toady alive that can catch a determined Corkman! The fair Miss Daunt – as stout-hearted as the best of 'em. By God, what! Oh these legal johnnies, they think they can sail closer to the wind than the rest of us. It ain't so. Certainly not. I know a trick worth two of that!' There was another five minutes of much the same kind of thing, the whole adding up to the fact that Admiral Somerville was proud to have served with every member of the committee and considered them all to be a capital crew.

Denis Hegarty, long since exhausted by so much unexpected

happiness, so much good food and so many big words, had curled up on a chair and fallen fast asleep. At long last cigars were lit and the conversation turned to other matters of importance – who was in at Admiralty house and the price of carriage horses, politics and Cuban cigars – and Ellen and Dónal were able to slip out and wander through the night-time streets as far as the quays. There they walked and talked above an hour, making their plans, talking about old friends, their past happinesses and sorrows.

They found themselves, in the end, standing looking down on a battered old fishing smack that reminded Dónal of his father's boat. A man who looked as old and battered his boat was sitting by a lantern on the afterdeck, contentedly smoking his pipe. The light of the lantern warmed the timbers of the deck and the stones of the quay and threw its reflection onto the still waters of the river.

'Good night skipper,' Dónal said. 'It was a bad day for the fishing.'

'Indeed it was,' the old man said. 'But a good night to be in harbour.'

'Did you ever hear tell of a boat called *Ellen Brice?*' Dónal enquired.

'I did,' the man said. 'That was the boat of a man by the name of Long. He died around about the year '95 or '96. Did you know him?'

'He was my father,' Dónal Long said.

The old man stood up and extended his hand for Dónal to shake. 'A decenter man never sailed a boat,' the old man said. 'And is it a sailor you are yourself?' Donal's clothes were battered and patched, but to a practised eye the remnants of a seaman's uniform were still visible.

'I am,' Dónal said. 'I'm captain of a trading schooner.' His heart leaped to say the words. 'And this is my bride-to-be.'

The old man shook hands with Ellen. 'Long life and happiness to you,' he said. Then his eyes took on a faraway look. 'A schooner. That'll be a fine ship. I remember a time I would have shipped aboard something like that myself. But I'm too old for that. But you, lady and gentleman, you have your whole life in front of you.'

As they walked back to the Oyster Tavern the tide was turning and a flurry of activity was breaking out. Ships, smacks, wherries, bumboats and every conceivable kind of vessel was making ready to leave the city docks and drop down the river with the ebb. They heard the calls of the mates and the chanting of the sailors as they hauled on the ropes that would swing them round. A fine brigantine was turning in front of them and Dónal heard the order to, 'Let go and haul!' and he tightened his grip on Ellen's arm. They watched the ship glide slowly down the stream into the deepening night, and they noticed that the cold rain and wind were gone and a few stars winked overhead. A full moon was rising above the eastern hills, a cool silver light changing everything.